Her heart stopped for what seemed an eternity...

...and then hammered hard to catch up as her head spun. She put a hand on the wall to steady herself.

"Claire," Joel said. His hat was sodden, and his shoulders were wet, too. He even had a drip of water hanging off the tip of his nose, and he wiped at it with the back of one hand. "I didn't know if it would really be you..."

"Joel," she whispered.

"Could I come in?" he asked. "It's, um, rather wet out here."

A gust of wind brought a wet slap with it as if to prove his point, and Claire finally stepped back to let him inside. Gloria and Ted looked up in mild curiosity.

"I know you weren't expecting me," he said quietly, keeping to Pennsylvania Dutch. "And I'm sorry if I'm an unpleasant surprise. I just... I was asking around about you, and when I heard that there was a basket weaver named Claire, I got my hopes up."

"You left," she said, her voice tight.

"*Yah.* There's a story there."

Patricia Johns is a *Publishers Weekly* bestselling author who writes from Alberta, Canada. She has her Hon. BA in English literature and currently writes for Harlequin's Love Inspired and Heartwarming lines. She also writes Amish romance for Kensington Books. You can find her at patriciajohns.com.

Books by Patricia Johns

Love Inspired

Amish Country Matches

The Amish Matchmaking Dilemma
Their Amish Secret

Redemption's Amish Legacies

The Nanny's Amish Family
A Precious Christmas Gift
Wife on His Doorstep
Snowbound with the Amish Bachelor
Blended Amish Blessings
The Amish Matchmaker's Choice

Harlequin Heartwarming

Amish Country Haven

A Deputy in Amish Country
A Cowboy in Amish Country
Her Amish Country Valentine

Visit the Author Profile page at LoveInspired.com for more titles.

Their Amish Secret

Patricia Johns

PLEASE RECYCLE
THIS PRODUCT IS RECYCLABLE

Recycling programs for this product may not exist in your area.

ISBN-13: 978-1-335-58644-5

Their Amish Secret

For questions and comments about the quality of this book, please contact us at CustomerService@Harlequin.com.

Love Inspired
22 Adelaide St. West, 41st Floor
Toronto, Ontario M5H 4E3, Canada
www.LoveInspired.com

Printed in U.S.A.

My grace is sufficient for thee:
for my strength is made perfect in weakness.
—*2 Corinthians* 12:9

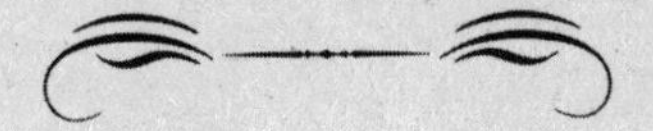

To my husband and son—
you're both at the center of my world. I love you!

Chapter One

Rain drummed on the roof and drove in sheets past the kitchen window. The weather report for Redemption, Pennsylvania, this week had called for rain, but it was coming down in buckets out there.

Claire Glick sat at the head of the table, her basket-weaving supplies in front of her. Today, she was teaching a middle-aged couple, Gloria and Ted Wassel, how to weave a simple basket using willow wands. She'd soaked the wands for six days and let them sit outside for one final day before her guests arrived. The wood was flexible now and perfect for weaving. This was Claire's special skill—creating useful, beautiful baskets.

"This is tough on the hands, isn't it?" Gloria rubbed her knuckles.

"It can be," Claire agreed. "I think my hands are used to it. But many people find the process therapeutic. You have to be very much in the present with your basket, and it helps to bring peace and calm to a troubled mind."

"I'd heard the same thing," Gloria said with a wistful smile cast in her husband's direction. Ted raised his bushy eyebrows but didn't say anything.

"You seem quite wise for being so young," Gloria said.

"People say that. I'm twenty-five." Claire smiled. It was her hard-won maturity that she was hoping would make Adel Knussli hire her full time as manager of the bed-and-breakfast. But she was still proving herself.

"Now, how do I do the rim again?" Gloria said.

"We twist the wand around the top and through this gap here—" Claire said.

Gloria leaned forward, as did her husband, and they both watched closely as Claire demonstrated the technique that created a lip around the edge of the basket. She tugged the wooden whip tight and pulled it hard into a V created by crossed wands.

"And then, once it's nice and tight, you

do—" Claire picked up the clippers and nipped off the last of the willow wand "—that. And then the next wand..."

Claire had found weaving provided peace for her own troubled mind when she was faced with those silent, lonely nights when her son was asleep. Aaron was conceived before she or his father were baptized into the Amish faith, and raising him alone hadn't been easy. Amish life wasn't set up for single mothers. Friends like Sarai Peachy, who was close to her age, were wonderful company during the days when she could find the time to socialize, but they weren't here in the evenings when she was left alone with her thoughts. Writing letters to her family only took up so much time, and when she'd put as much into words as she cared to, she'd sit down with willow wands, or grape vines, straw or even water reeds, and she'd start to create something beautiful. It soothed her mind—gave her something to do with her hands when she seemed most apt to travel down memory lane and go over her regrets one by one.

Claire could hear the sound of the dog's toenails against the floorboards upstairs, and Aaron's footsteps, too, as she twisted the second wand around, pushed it through the gap and pulled on it hard to give it a tight fit. Then she clipped it off and handed the basket back to Gloria for her to continue. Gloria took the next wand and bent it the same way. She had caught on to the process quickly, like a natural.

Claire's four-year-old son came down the stairs, a big German shepherd trailing closely behind. Normally during her basket-weaving classes, Aaron would go outside to play, but the downpour made that impossible, so instead she had her little boy, the dog at his side, peering at the *Englisher* couple's work.

"That one needs to be tighter, right, *Mamm*?" Aaron pointed at one of the wands Ted had twisted over the top of his basket.

"*Yah*, a little tighter," Claire agreed, then she added in Pennsylvania Dutch, "But I told you to let me teach my students in peace."

"Sorry." Aaron sighed. He turned his attention to the dog. "Goliath, sit."

"Goliath" simply looked at him.

"Sit, Goliath."

"His name is Ollie, remember?" Claire put a spare wand onto the counter. "We have to return him to his owners."

"He's Goliath to me." Aaron looked plaintively over at the German shepherd.

The dog wandered away toward the window and put his nose up next to the glass. Goliath was a stray they'd found on the property of Draschel Bed and Breakfast two weeks ago. He didn't seem to know Pennsylvania Dutch, which made no difference to Aaron, who chattered at him in Dutch anyway. Goliath had grown rather fond of Aaron, and Aaron had become attached to the dog.

"Do we really have to give him back?" Aaron asked for the umpteenth time.

"*Yah.* The owners put out the flyer, and they want their dog back. I'll call the number this evening at the phone booth and tell them we've found him." Claire turned her attention back to Gloria and switched to English again. "Nicely done! You're almost finished. And Ted, that looks very good, too."

Ted's basket wasn't quite so straight as his wife's. His was more lopsided, so Claire took hold of it and gave it a strong twist to even it out. Basket weaving was a skill that required muscle and an unshakable belief in one's own vision. Perhaps that was why it appealed to her so much. In the Amish world, a woman should be soft, gentle. In basket weaving, she got to experiment with the tougher side of her nature.

There was a knock on the door, and Claire handed Ted back his basket with a smile and headed over to answer it. Her mind was still on the Wassels and their basket making. She opened the door and gave a polite smile to the man standing on her step. A hitched buggy stood with the horse under the stable shelter behind him, and he was already drenched from the downpour.

He was Amish—tall, lean, and with one arm looking noticeably thinner than the other. For a moment, she didn't know who he was, and she was about to step back, ushering him inside out of the rain. It was then that she noticed a scar over one eyebrow. She dragged her gaze back up to his face, and she recognized him now. It was him—Joel Beiler—albeit much changed.

Her heart stopped for what seemed an eternity and then hammered hard to catch up as her head spun. She put a hand on the wall to steady herself.

"Claire." Joel's hat was sodden, and his shoulders were wet, too. He even had a drip of water hanging off the tip of his nose. "I didn't know if it would really be you..."

"Joel," she whispered.

"Could I come in?" He wiped the drip off his nose with back of his hand. "It's...um... rather wet out here."

A gust of wind brought a wet slap with it as if to prove his point, and Claire finally stepped back to let him inside. Gloria and Ted looked up in mild curiosity.

"I know you weren't expecting me," he said quietly, keeping to Pennsylvania Dutch. "And I'm sorry if I'm an unpleasant surprise. I just... I was asking around about you, and when I heard that there was a basket weaver named Claire, I got my hopes up."

"You left," she said, her voice tight.

"*Yah.* There's a story there."

There must be, because he hardly looked like the muscular, jocular Joel the other young men had called "a quarter horse of a man" whom she remembered from five years ago. This man was thin, almost like he'd missed too many meals, and he had a limp and one arm that seemed to respond sluggishly. That wasn't the powerful man she remembered.

Joel's gaze moved over to Aaron, who eyed

him curiously. Goliath's hackles went up, and he let out a low growl.

"I'm teaching a class," she said abruptly. "I need to finish with them before we discuss anything."

"Right, right..." Joel paused. "Of course. I could just have a seat by the stove."

He waited for her to nod permission, then headed over to the woodstove and held his hands out to it. Water from his hat dripped onto the stove top, hissing as it turned into steam. Claire sucked in a stabilizing breath. Goliath—or Ollie, but they'd been calling him Goliath for two weeks before she found the flyer—set himself solidly between Aaron and the new arrival, and Claire felt a little bit better about their overprotective canine guest.

Claire went over to the table and rejoined Gloria and Ted.

"It's looking very good!" Claire said, forcing some cheer into her voice and handing the clippers to Ted. Her hands trembled, and she hoped it wasn't noticeable. "Now, just snip off the ends."

Ted did as she told him, and he smiled as he looked at his finished result. Claire stole a peek over at Joel, who stood by the stove still, his back to her. He had all his weight on one leg—his good leg. She could tell that he favored one side of his body, and one hand hung at his side in an almost limp fashion. But then he clenched a fist, as if he could feel her gaze on it.

"Basket weaving is quite the experience," Ted said. "My wife has been asking to take one of your classes for months, and I'm glad we finally did it. Thank you for giving us this opportunity, Claire."

Ted's attention moved toward the window, where the storm had not let up. The sky was growing darker by the minute. Gloria clipped the last of her willow wands and set the basket down on the table, looking at it from one side and then the other.

Joel glanced over his shoulder and met Claire's gaze. She felt her face heat, and she looked away from him.

"This is amazing, Claire," Gloria said. "I have to agree with my husband. This has been a real treat. You've made this such a great experience."

Claire smiled. "I'm glad. The baskets are yours, of course, and I'm so glad you enjoyed your time with me today. I have some baked goods to go home with you." She scooped up two plastic bags that contained a few cookies each and brownies. She put them into their baskets with a smile she hoped looked natural.

"Oh, thank you!" Gloria said. "How sweet of you. This is really great. Ted, we should probably start home, don't you think? This storm is so much worse than the weather channel called for."

Everyone looked toward the window then, and Ted reached for his coat hanging on a hook.

"I think we should, Gloria. Thank you again, Claire! We'll give you some shining reviews online."

"And we'll tell all our friends about this place." Gloria grabbed the baskets.

They put on their jackets and picked up a big umbrella they'd shared when they arrived. They pressed their shoulders together as they ducked outside, then the umbrella popped up over their heads. Claire smiled and held the door as the couple pushed out into the driving rain. Her gaze moved toward Joel's buggy and horse, still hitched, standing underneath the protective shelter attached to the stable. The Wassels jumped into their car, and the headlights came on as it rumbled to life. They waved, and she waved back, then shut the door as they started to back up.

Claire slowly turned.

"You teach basket weaving now?" Joel asked.

"I do."

"You always did make beautiful baskets."

"*Yah*, there's a market for it." Her voice sounded breathy in her own ears. She swallowed and turned to her son. "Aaron, sweetie, can you take Goliath upstairs and play in your room for a while?"

"You called him Goliath." Aaron shot her a victorious smile.

"I did, but it doesn't change that he still doesn't rightfully belong to us, son," she said firmly. "Now, upstairs to play, please."

"Can I have a brownie?" he asked.

Claire handed him a plastic baggie with a brownie inside. "Don't leave crumbs."

She said it more out of habit than actual thought.

"Goliath eats the crumbs." Aaron smiled and mounted the stairs, the dog loyally following behind him. Goliath might not answer to the name or know Pennsylvania Dutch, but he had settled on Aaron as his human of choice.

When Claire heard her son's footsteps grow fainter, she met Joel's gaze, and her strength seemed to seep out of her. Joel Beiler…on her doorstep. How many times had she thought about this possibility as she lay in bed at night, imagining this very scenario?

"Why now?" She leaned weakly against the counter. "You promised me you'd be back within a matter of weeks five years ago. And you never came. I waited and waited, and I *believed* you'd come. Month after month! I faced my community's censure. I faced my parents' disappointment when I was pregnant and had no husband…and you were just gone!"

Joel's gaze flickered toward the stairs. "I heard that the Claire Glick who made baskets had a little boy. I wasn't sure…"

"*Yah*, he's yours. I gave birth to our son, and I kept looking my neighbors in the face, all the while knowing they were using me as a morality tale for their children. At least I wasn't baptized yet, so I didn't get shunned, but I did it all alone! And *now* you come back?"

"I didn't know you were pregnant," he said.

"So, if I hadn't been carrying your baby, you disappearing would have been fine?" She shook her head. "You promised to marry me, Joel! You said you'd never loved anyone like me before. You said you couldn't imagine spending your life with any other woman. You said a lot of things…and it counted for nothing."

And somehow, deep in those dark eyes, she still saw the same Joel of five years ago—handsome, funny, strong…and maybe just a little too good to be true, because he hadn't lived up to any of it.

"So he is my son." Joel's eyes suddenly misted.

"Do you think I'm the type of woman to have had a son by someone else?" she demanded. "*Yah*, he's yours! But I won't be telling him that."

"I heard enough about you that I was relatively certain…" His chin trembled slightly. "And the timing…it added up. You said his name is Aaron?"

"*Yah*. Aaron."

"Are you two okay?" Joel asked. "Do you have enough?"

"The owner of this bed-and-breakfast is allowing me to run it temporarily," Claire said. "If she allows me to be the permanent, live-in manager, then yes, I'll be fine. What I make from basket-weaving classes and managing this place will take care of us."

"Maybe I could stay for a day or two," Joel said. "I could pay for a few nights here at the bed-and-breakfast. We have a lot to catch up on, and I'd like to get to know my son."

He wanted to get to know Aaron, and then he'd leave…like Goliath was going to leave, too. Aaron was saying too many goodbyes already in his young life, and she wouldn't put him through an unnecessary one. Her heartbreak over this man didn't have to be Aaron's, too.

"No." She shook her head.

"Oh…" Joel licked his lips. He seemed to have expected a different answer. "Is there any way I can come by and see the two of you again? I know you're angry with me, Claire, but for Aaron's sake."

"This *is* for Aaron's sake!" she snapped. "Aaron knows he doesn't have a father, and he's made his peace with that. I'm not going to confuse him now."

Joel nodded. "I probably deserve that."

"You definitely deserve it," she retorted.

Claire saw headlights sweep back up the drive, but her heart was pounding in her ears.

"I didn't want to leave you, Claire," he said. "I did love you. I need you to know that."

Footsteps sounded on the steps, and there

was a knock. She numbly walked over to the door and pulled it open. The Wassels stood there on the step, their umbrella over their heads.

"A huge tree went down over the road," Ted said. "It looks like lightning struck it. We aren't going to be able to get past until someone is able to clear it."

The bed-and-breakfast was located on a dead-end country road that lead to the highway. That one exit was the only one. If the Wassels couldn't make it out, then neither could Joel. Sending him away wasn't going to be an option. The timing couldn't be worse.

"Could we stay here for a little while?" Gloria asked hopefully.

Claire pushed back her surging emotions and pasted a smile onto her face. These were her clients, the ones who paid good money to have a cheerful Amish woman teach them a skill.

"Of course, of course." Claire ushered them inside. "Come back in. I'll put on some tea."

And when she looked over at Joel, she saw those same, familiar dark eyes that used to make her melt...but the rest of him was so very changed. The muscular bulk from outdoor work was gone. Whatever had happened to Joel Beiler? And what was she going to do with him until this storm passed?

Joel held his hands out toward the stove. The *Englisher* couple came inside, rubbing their hands together. It was a cold rain—like winter didn't quite want to let go, after all. He saw Aaron and the dog come back down the stairs, and the boy sat on a step, watching the adults silently. His gaze moved over to Joel, and Joel smiled and nodded at him. The boy smiled back.

His son… He'd had no idea he'd fathered a child with Claire. Their romance had been a whirlwind, and he'd fallen headlong in love with her. Yes, they'd also gone too far, and he'd regretted those actions ever after, because he'd made promises and then acted like a husband when he wasn't one yet. He'd meant it when he said he was coming back for her, but then he'd had the first stroke that left him debilitated in the hospital. It had taken months to learn how to talk again, to walk, to feed himself. And he'd honestly thought that Claire would be better off with another man—a more worthy man. Because he was now a serious liability.

But Aaron's clear, blue-eyed gaze tied Joel's heart up into knots. *His son.* Joel's mother had told him he'd been blond when he was little, with hair like afternoon sunlight. So did his son.

Claire brought a filled kettle over to the woodstove. She used a lid lifter to pull a round lid off the top of the stove, revealing orange fire beneath, and she put the kettle on top. Her arm brushed against his, and he restrained himself from reaching out to touch her hand.

"If a tree is down, I might be here for a little while, too," he said quietly.

Claire looked up at him. Her eyes looked different than before. There was more experience in her gaze, less hopeful sparkle. That was his fault, wasn't it?

"*Yah*, you might be."

"You mind if I put my horse in your stable?" He knew her well enough to be certain she'd never let an animal suffer discomfort.

Claire paused, then angled her head to one side in acceptance. "Might as well."

"Thank you."

"*Yah*, sure." She moved away again, and Joel headed back over toward the door. The *Englisher* couple smiled at him.

"You won't get far," the man said.

"I'm just getting my horse into the stable," he replied.

"Are you?" The man brightened. "You want help?"

Joel shrugged. "Sure."

These *Englisher* tourists were enthralled by the most basic chores, it seemed, but the man seemed genuinely interested, and Joel couldn't resent him for that. Joel pulled on his boots.

"There's another pair of rubber boots there, Ted," Claire said. "They're a men's size ten. Feel free to use them."

There was a pair of men's boots sitting on a mat, and Ted—because that appeared to be his name—pulled them on. He grabbed the umbrella again, and Joel pulled his collar up. Joel looked over his shoulder, and he found Claire and Aaron looking at him. Five years ago, it would have been a dream come true to have a child with Claire, but nothing had turned out the way he'd hoped back then.

Joel opened the door, and they plunged out into the storm. The umbrella seemed to work just fine for the first few yards, and then a gust of wind whipped it inside out, and Joel helped the older man wrestle it back in shape, and then shut it.

"No use, I guess," Ted said as they dashed underneath the covered overhang next to the stable. Ted left the umbrella leaning against the wall, and Joel limped over to the horse's side and started unbuckling straps. A flash of lightning lit up the sky, and then a heartbeat later there was a deafening boom. The horse nickered and shuffled his hooves uneasily, and Joel put a reassuring hand on his sleek neck.

"It's okay, big fellow," he said in Pennsylvania Dutch. "Storms pass."

Ted stepped forward and started undoing buckles on the other side, and when Joel looked at him in surprise, he said, "I grew up on a farm not far from here."

"Amish?"

"No, just a regular old farm boy. But I know the drill."

"Ah."

It didn't take long to get the horse unhitched, and Joel led him into the stable and got him settled with hay in a stall next to another horse, and then he picked up a brush.

"So you like basket weaving?" Joel picked some straw out of the brush bristles.

"My wife likes basket weaving," Ted replied with a short laugh. "In fact, this is the first time she's woven a basket, but she's watched a hundred YouTube videos about it."

Joel smiled faintly and gave one last strong brushstroke to his horse's side before he put the brush back on the shelf and patted his horse's muscled shoulder affectionately.

"You'll be okay now," Joel said to the horse.

"Do you have a guess at how long it'll take to get that tree chopped up and moved?" Ted asked.

How long indeed. Joel was hoping it wouldn't be done too quickly, because the longer it took, the more time he had here with his son—and with Claire. He knew he had nothing to offer her besides some money, but to gain some of her good opinion would make him feel better.

"It depends on when the rain stops," Joel replied. "No one is coming out to do it in this weather."

Ted looked toward the door, his brow furrowed. *Yah*, Joel had similar worries. He'd had plans to head back to his hotel room in the town of Redemption tonight. Would Claire even let him stay under her roof? Or would he be bunking in the stable with his horse?

"This is a bed-and-breakfast," Joel added.

As far as the *Englishers* were concerned, at least.

"Yeah, yeah... We'll probably have to stay a few days. We just didn't pack for it."

Joel led the way back out to the covered area where the buggy waited, and he pulled out his own travel bag.

"I wasn't planning on staying, either, but I think if we pull together, we'll all be okay," Joel said. "That's how we Amish do it."

"My wife will appreciate that." Ted squinted at the blowing rain.

"Is this a special occasion for you?" Joel guessed.

"The opposite," Ted replied. "This is the anniversary of our oldest son's death. He died in a boating accident. The last few years we've made a point of getting away, doing something different. It's avoidance."

"I'm sorry."

Another jagged line of lightning lit up the sky, and the boom sent a shiver down Joel's spine. That was close. It was the kind of lightning strike that could fell a tree. The older man seemed to rally himself.

"I'd appreciate it if you didn't bring it up to my wife, though," Ted said. "This is a tough time for her. Maybe it's best we're stuck out here in Amish Country a little longer, after all."

"I won't say anything." The wind seemed to pause for a moment, and Joel nodded toward the house. "Let's go."

Times like this he wished he didn't have half his body responding so sluggishly. It was like having a leg that was asleep—always doing half of what his brain told it to do. After five years of recovering, this was an improvement, but he still remembered what normal felt like. Wind slammed like a wet sheet against him, and his boot caught on the rocky ground, his foot not lifting as high as he meant to lift it. He hopped twice, regaining his balance, and he felt that old rush of frustration.

He used to be strong, athletic and capable. Now, he'd lost a lot of that.

Ted looked back, and Joel pretended nothing had happened, relieved to grab hold of the handrail that led up to the side door. Ted went inside the house first, and Joel followed him, slamming the door shut behind them. They both dripped puddles on the linoleum floor as they peeled off their coats.

"Ted!" Gloria said. "I can't believe you did that!"

"It's just rain, Gloria." Ted straightened his shoulders a little.

Joel and Ted went to the stove again, and Claire handed each of them a towel. Gloria tutted and helped Ted wrap his around his shoulders, but Claire just handed Joel his mutely.

Joel caught Claire's eye, a smile tickling one side of his lips, but she didn't return it. He shook the towel open and wrapped it around his own shoulders. The warmth was welcome.

"I doubt that tree is going anywhere today." Claire looked out the window. "Ted and Gloria, you're welcome to stay the night here. We have bedrooms, hot water and more than enough food to keep us all fed."

She hadn't mentioned him, Joel noticed.

"Thank you so much, Claire," Gloria said. "We'll pay, of course."

Claire shook her head. "This isn't a vacation. Don't worry about that."

"And it isn't free for you, either," Gloria said. "I insist. We're happy to pay the going rate for a room here while we stay."

Joel noticed that she didn't argue any further. Ted moved off to the table with his wife, and Claire came back to the stove to fill her teapot from the steaming kettle.

"Am I permitted to stay, too?" he asked quietly.

"I don't see any other way around it." The earlier chill to her tone seemed to be gone. "But we need to have an agreement."

"All right."

"You don't tell Aaron who you are." She met his gaze. "I don't want him to know. Not right now, at least. So as far as Aaron is concerned, you are only a traveling Amish man. That's all. And you're staying here until that tree is removed from the road."

"Are you and I going to have a chance to talk?"

"Maybe."

She was angry, it seemed, and five years was a long time to let something stew. Getting her to talk to him openly might take more time than he had here.

"Claire, I do have an explanation for you," he said. "I'm not asking for you to take me back, or even forgive me. Trust me, I'm not here for that. But an explanation might help you feel better about everything. You never know."

Claire paused and looked at him. Her eyes were filled with misgiving.

"You didn't come for that?"

He shook his head. "No."

"Oh… Oh… Right." She looked away, and he thought he saw her cheeks color. He was embarrassing her.

"Claire, I had good reason for what I did," he said. "And I didn't know about our son. But I did come find you for a good reason, too."

She turned back toward him. "Which is?"

"My *daet* died. And I got an inheritance. I wanted to see if Aaron was mine, and if he was, I was going to sign that inheritance over to you."

Claire blinked. "What?"

"It's the least I can do," he said. "It's not a huge amount of money, but it's what I've got. I left you alone while you struggled to raise our child. But I can provide you something now."

"That's…that's really kind of you, Joel."

"It's half-decent of me," he said. "Let's not exaggerate things. I also caused you a world of grief the last five years, and this might help to make up for some of it."

"Thank you," she said quietly.

"When this storm lets up, I'll go to the bank and get you a money order," he said. "Maybe having me around for a day or so might not be quite so bothersome that way."

Claire's expression softened. "It's a shock to see you again, is all."

"*Yah*..." He hadn't written or given her any warning on purpose. He doubted she'd want to see him given the time to think it over. And if Aaron was his, he'd wanted to at least get a chance to meet his son.

"But I was serious about what I said earlier," she said. "I don't want Aaron to know anything. Okay? Not a word."

"Not a word."

Joel wasn't going to be able to buy his way back into her life, or his son's. Not that he was trying, but it was good to know all the same.

Claire stood up and went to the kitchen window. She squinted and leaned forward.

"It's not going to stop," she said. "And Old Jack is out there, still."

"Who?"

"Our old quarter horse. He likes it out there, and if it's just a passing storm, we leave him. But this is bad. I have to go get him."

Joel looked past her, out the window at the pouring rain. "I'll do it."

"No, you stay and get dry," she said. "I'll go."

Stay and get dry, like he was some feeble old man. No, Joel wouldn't be doing anything of the sort.

"I said I'd help you." He reached for his sodden coat on the hook. "I'm already wet. A little more rain isn't going to hurt anything."

While he was here, he'd help. He could do that much.

Chapter Two

Claire looked over her shoulder at the Wassels. That entire conversation had been in Pennsylvania Dutch. Aaron had found himself a glass of milk and stood by the icebox drinking it. Goliath wandered over to the door and looked over at them meaningfully.

Claire went over and opened it for him. The dog looked out into the downpour for a moment, then stepped outside, keeping close to the house. He did his business and came back inside in record time, giving his fur a shake and spraying everything with a mist of rainwater.

"Aaron, you stay here with our guests," Claire said in English so that they'd understand. "I need to go get Old Jack."

"He's out in the rain," Aaron said, suddenly perking up. "But he likes rain."

"He won't like this much of it," Claire said. "You stay put, okay?"

"Yah, Mamm."

"Can we help?" Gloria asked.

"No, no," Claire reassured her. "We won't be long."

The last thing Claire needed was tourists underfoot. She'd bring Old Jack in, and then they'd be able to shut everything up tight and ride out the storm. Besides, if she was asking Adel to let her run this place, it included caring for the animals when their part-time helper, Trevor, wasn't around to pitch in. Claire knew the job.

Joel waited for her at the door, and she slipped her coat on over her dress, then pulled the hood up.

"Where is the horse?" Joel asked.

"He's normally in the shelter of the trees at the back pasture," she said. "I don't want to leave him out there with lightning, though." Lightning strikes that killed animals didn't happen often, but they did occur.

Joel opened the door and plunged outside ahead her. Claire followed, and as she watched his limping gait, she wondered if he'd meant it. Was he really going to hand his inheritance over to her? It was almost too generous to be true, because he'd need that money, too, wouldn't he? Especially after whatever had injured him?

She pulled the door solidly shut behind her and closed her eyes as a rush of rain blew straight into her face. So much for the hood.

"Wait!" she called, jogging after Joel. She caught up with him at the gate that led into the pasture. The ground was already waterlogged, and her boots sank into the sod.

"*Yah?*" Joel turned.

"Old Jack is a moody horse. He doesn't like just anyone."

Joel put his hand up to shade his view through the rain.

"Let me go first, at least," she said and she stepped past him, through the gate, and started out across the field.

The field was even wetter than the lawn, and she sank into a puddle that turned out to be mud at the bottom. She hauled her boot out with a squelch and pushed forward. The field had started to flood. A rumble of thunder overhead sent a shiver down her arms, and she took another step, only to sink deeper into the pooling water.

The trees weren't too far ahead, and Old Jack stood beneath them as he usually did during storms. She saw his ears flick at the thunder.

"Hey."

She startled to find Joel at her side. He was taller than she was, and his boots, being men's, went higher up his leg.

"Go back," he said, and not waiting for her response, he plunged past her across the sodden field. His boots sucked into muddy water, too, but he was able to go farther than she had, even with his limp.

Claire stood there in the mud, her heart pounding. This wasn't as helpful as he thought. She was trying to prove to herself, and ultimately to Adel, that she could take care of things on her own.

Are you proving a point, Gott? she prayed. *Of all people, I don't want his help!*

But Joel pushed on. His left leg didn't seem as strong as his right, and he leaned all his weight to the side to pull his boot up. How long could he manage that?

She looked around, seeing higher ground several yards to the left, and she struggled in that direction. Another boom of thunder made Old Jack rear up and whinny, and Claire hurried on. She climbed up to higher ground, but the slight ledge led in the wrong direction, away from the horse. She stood there, wind and rain whipping around her as Joel carefully pushed forward. She could just make him out, a blurry figure, as he slowed, stopped, leaned forward to rest his hands on his knees. He was tiring.

She could still see a shadow of the man from five years ago in the thinner, limping man across that field. The persistence was there still. But five years ago, he'd been all muscle and strength, built for hard work and success. He'd captured her heart with one of his direct looks, and she'd been smitten. It hadn't just been his physique that drew her in—he'd been gentle and funny, too, but she'd certainly appreciated his good looks.

Had that been shallow of her, considering just how long those looks lasted on any of them? It was a lesson the young learned sooner or later.

Joel was a different man now, but there was still a part of her heart that yearned for him like it used to. Claire should stop that, though. She was wiser now. She'd been a foolish young woman back then, trusting a man's poetic declarations of love before he moved on to a new farm to work. He said he'd be back in three weeks.

Had there been other girls on other farms that he'd sweet-talked, too? It stood to reason there would be. She'd come to the conclusion a long time ago that what she'd felt so sincerely had been little more than a game for him.

She pulled the hood of her coat farther over her head and watched as Joel straightened and continued on as a boom of thunder rumbled across the sky. He reached Old Jack, and the horse shied away from him, backing into the trees. Another wall of wind and rain hit Claire, and she ducked her head against the drenching blow. When she opened her eyes, Joel had caught the horse by his bridle, and he jumped, trying to pull himself up onto the horse's back, but his left leg wouldn't lift high enough. He dropped back down the ground.

She held her breath, waiting, and then she saw Joel grab a fistful of mane and he pulled again. Inch by inch, he rose higher until he flopped his torso over Old Jack's back, and by some small mercy, the horse stood still. It took another couple of minutes for Joel to get his bad leg over the horse, and then he was upright. Slowly, he rode the horse out of the trees, and Old Jack easily plodded through the water and mud, going in the familiar direction of the stable.

Claire turned and headed in the same direction, pushing through the rain with one arm up to block what she could of the cold, whipping drops from hitting her face. She met Joel at the stable entrance. He slid off the horse's back to the ground, and as his left boot hit the ground, his knee buckled underneath his weight.

She hurried forward and caught him under one arm—what good that did. He fell anyway, slipping from her grip. He lay there for a moment, then pushed himself up to a seated position with her hand still under his arm, and he fixed her with an annoyed look.

"What are you going to do, lift me?" he asked irritably.

True. She couldn't lift him, and the gesture had been more instinct than logic. Claire let go of him and stepped back, and Joel shifted his weight to his good side and rose awkwardly to his feet once more. His left leg and hip were covered in mud.

"I'm fine," Joel said before she could say anything. "I'm not completely useless."

"I didn't say that." Claire resisted the urge to help any further.

"*Yah*, well..." Joel's limp was worse now, and she opened the door. Old Jack didn't need any more encouragement to go inside the warm stable. Claire and Joel followed him inside, and she pulled the door solidly shut behind them.

The stable was warm from the animals' body heat, and it smelled of fresh hay. The other two horses were chewing on some oats contentedly. One stall was filled with fresh bales of hay and silage. The stable was watertight and dry and on high enough ground that it should stay that way.

"Thank you for getting him," Claire said as she led the big horse to the far stall.

She looked back at Joel. He leaned against the rail, wincing. He'd hurt himself when he came off the horse, but he seemed sensitive about that, so she wouldn't mention it again.

"I haven't seen a storm this bad this time of year...ever," she added.

"I've seen a couple. Ohio is worse."

Ohio was where Claire was from—where she'd met Joel. It seemed strange to have him mentioning Ohio weather offhand like that. He wasn't from Ohio. He'd just been there for the work.

Claire picked up a horse brush and an old towel and began wiping mud off Old Jack's sides and legs. The horse stood placidly as she worked.

"Let me help you." When Joel moved closer, Old Jack laid his ears back.

"No, it's better that I do it."

Joel nodded, but he didn't leave. He just stood there watching her work.

"I've had years to think it over," Claire said. "And I know my own mistakes. I made plenty. But you should never have said what you didn't mean. I believed you."

"I didn't lie to you," he said.

Joel was going to stand by those flimsy declarations of love even now? Even after he'd abandoned her the way he had? Maybe she shouldn't be surprised. He probably thought he did nothing wrong. People had a way of convincing themselves they were the innocent party.

"It took me years to accept that you didn't love me," Claire said. "I had to do a lot of searching of my own heart, seeing where I was too naive, seeing my own mistakes. And I finally accepted that you had lied to me."

"I didn't lie."

"You didn't come back, either!" Claire put a reassuring hand on Old Jack's big chest and moved under his head to the other side of him. "I'd made my peace with what I thought you'd done, and you're about to ruin that for me, aren't you?"

"Would you rather just think I'm awful?"

Claire continued to wipe the mud and rain from the horse's high shoulder. Maybe she did want to believe he was awful—it was easier. But she'd always wonder if she didn't let him tell her the whole story. Her curiosity was stronger than her pride.

"All right," she said. "What happened? You got hurt or something. You've got the limp. A horse accident?"

"I had a really bad stroke."

She frowned. She hadn't expected that. "That isn't common in someone so young."

"It isn't," he agreed. "It turns out that I have a condition that makes my blood cells stick together and clot up. Those clots can get lodged in my arteries, and this particular one ended up in my brain. It caused a debilitating stroke." He pulled a small bottle out of his breast pocket and shook it. "I have to take these now every day. I have enough for three more weeks, in case you're worried."

She had been, just for a moment. It was pure instinct. "You should have sent word to me from the hospital."

"I couldn't," he said, his voice low. "I couldn't feed myself, walk or even talk. It took months and months of rehab to get back my ability to lift my hand to my mouth or say so much as a coherent word. And this—" he gestured toward himself "—this is after years of therapy. I still trip sometimes—as you've seen. The left side of my body just won't do what it used to."

"You should have told me when you were able," she repeated. "I was waiting."

He was silent, his jaw clenched. It made his mouth into a crooked line across his face—the right side straight and firm and the left sagging just a bit.

"Now I know about Aaron, and that changes things," he said. "But let's pretend that we hadn't conceived a baby that summer. You knew me for a matter of weeks. I was just some ranch hand who took you on walks and told you he thought you were pretty..."

"You said more than that," she murmured. They'd certainly done more than that, and she'd gone to *Gott* for forgiveness for it.

You're beautiful, Claire. I've never felt this way before. It's like you fill up a part of my heart that's never been touched.

"I meant every word of what I said." He

took off his hat and let it drip onto the floor next to him. "But I was just some worker… and when I ended up unable to control even my bodily functions for months, was that really the man you wanted to marry after all?"

The thought of him helpless in some hospital bed as his muscles melted off his body was enough to make her throat tight.

"You didn't give me the choice."

"I didn't inflict that choice on you," he replied, his voice firming. "I did the right thing with the information I had, and you can't convince me otherwise. I know Aaron makes it different, but I didn't know about him. I thought for sure you'd be married to someone else the next year—someone strong and capable. You deserved that."

Claire hung the towel over the top rail of the stall and turned back toward him. "When you were struggling in the hospital, you didn't want me by your side, did you?"

She fixed him with a direct gaze. She needed to see his answer as well as hear it. For her own ability to sort this out in her own heart.

"I didn't want you there," he agreed. "I didn't want anyone to see me like that. It was humiliating."

She nodded. That was the honest truth of it—he hadn't longed for her to be there next to him. When life got hard, he'd preferred to be alone.

"The thing is, I have a lifelong condition," Joel went on. "I take medication to manage it, but there is always a very real risk that the same thing will happen again. I might die, or I might end up bedridden for the rest of my natural days. I might be unable to talk or even clean myself. I pray *Gott* just takes me, if it comes down to that. But even after I recovered from that stroke—as much as I did—I couldn't offer myself to you. Not like this. I'm not the same man I was. I'm not as strong—I'm not able to work like I used to. And I come with a lifetime of risk."

Claire could see that, but the risk that surrounded him was more than his medical condition. She'd given this man her heart, and he'd crushed it.

"What do you do for work now?" she asked. It wouldn't be ranch work anymore—not the way he looked.

"I learned how to do basic bookkeeping for Amish businesses," he said. "So I do that in Indiana, where my family is."

"Are you…engaged or…" She forced herself to look up. Was there a woman who'd been willing to take on that lifetime of risk with him? Someone else he'd felt was more worthy than she was? Maybe his excuses were his way of letting her down easy.

"No. No fiancée. No girlfriend. Nothing like that."

She nodded. So he was truly single. Maybe that could take away some of the sting.

"What about you?" he asked. "Do you have a boyfriend or…"

"I have a prospect." Claire took the horse brush and turned back to the job in front of her. "Being a single mother has made finding a husband very difficult for me, but my move to Redemption was probably the best thing I could have done. My cousin Zedechiah is the bishop here. So my association with him… helps. He speaks for me, and people have gotten to know my character."

"You have a prospect, you said?"

She looked over at him again, and she noticed how his interest was suddenly piqued. Jealousy? As if he had any right!

"There's a matchmaker here in Redemption," Claire said, turning back to the brushing. "Adel Knussli. She set up a possible match for me—an Amish farmer in Oregon.

She knows his second cousin, and several people speak well of him. He's looking for a wife, and even knowing my situation, he asked if he could write me a letter."

"And?" Joel frowned.

"And what?"

"Did you write him back?"

"Not yet."

"Can I see what he wrote?"

She jerked in surprise. "No! Why would you even ask that? Joel, you and I are nothing to each other anymore! If I write letters with a man in Oregon, that's my business."

"Maybe there's something I'll notice in him that seems…off," he said.

Was it so unbelievable that a farmer somewhere might be interested in her?

"What? Because I'm a single mother, that's all I can expect—a man with something glaringly wrong with him?" she snapped. Old Jack shuffled in response to her outburst, and she forced herself to calm.

"No," Joel said. "Because I care about who you end up giving your heart to. I know how precious that is."

His words slipped past her armor, and she felt her cheeks warm. Those were the kinds of words that used to make her swoon, but

Claire didn't turn around. Words and actions were two different things. She put the brush back on the ledge.

"You are right," Joel said after a moment of silence. "It's not my place to ask about that. I'm glad you have a prospect. But he'd be my son's new *daet*."

There was that. Joel hadn't known about his son, and when he learned of his existence, he'd come. She could give him that much.

"He's thirty," Claire said. "So older than me, but not by too much. His wife died four years ago, and he has a little girl who needs a *mamm*."

This man in Oregon had experienced pain and heartbreak, too. Perhaps his hardships had done the same maturing for him as hers had done in her life. That was her hope—to find someone who might understand.

Joel nodded. "I see. So he's young, too. And probably strong and able-bodied."

"*Yah*. And a sister for Aaron would be very nice. Aaron gets lonely on his own so much." She let herself out of the stall and headed over to the oat bin to refill Old Jack's bucket. "But having you here—that might change things. Adel told him that I was a woman who'd been done wrong. That I'd been taken advantage of. That I was a good mother, but I was very single and there was no man who would come asking after me."

She dumped the oats into the bucket and returned the scoop.

"I would ruin that," Joel said.

She turned back toward him. "*Yah*, you would. Like any man, he doesn't want complication. He wants his wife to be his and only his."

Joel was silent for a moment, then he sighed. "Are you asking me to go away and never lay eyes on Aaron again?"

Claire opened her mouth, and she wished she could bring the words out to confirm exactly that, but she couldn't say it. Joel was here. He might not have come for her, but he did care about his child.

"I don't know what I'm asking of you," she admitted. "You're right that Aaron changes things. I can see that. But a woman in my position doesn't have a lot of options."

"I'd be cruel to ruin yours," he said quietly.

She nodded, and a lump rose in her throat. Why did he have to come back now?

"For what it's worth, Claire, I'm really sorry for having left you alone in raising our son." He reached out and caught her fingers in his. His touch was so familiar that her heart skipped a beat. She pulled her hand free. That wasn't a promise to keep clear of her prospects, was it?

"You probably won't want to leave me that inheritance money if I end up getting married, will you?" she asked.

"Do you want to marry this man?"

Claire sighed. Did she? It was a shock to know that she even had the option, but did she want to marry a man who might be strict with Aaron? Did she want to put her life into the hands of a man she hardly knew in a state she'd never seen?

"My original plan was to get the job of running this place," Claire said. "The matchmaker owns this bed-and-breakfast, and her sister used to run it before she got married. I was hoping to live here and run the business for her. It would be a safe, secure place to raise my little boy, and I wouldn't have to marry for that kind of security. That mattered to me."

Joel met her gaze, then nodded. "You want options. You don't want to be pushed into anything."

She wanted her own options, yes, but she also wanted to protect her boy. Aaron was a sweet child, but he'd been raised by a mother alone, and he wouldn't be used to a stepfather's expectations.

"I don't want a stepfather to be harsh with Aaron," she said. "I care who gets to be his *daet*, too."

Joel nodded, and he dropped his gaze.

"I came to give you the money. My conscience wouldn't leave me alone until I determined to do it. It's yours. And you can decide what you will about your future. It can help give you that freedom so you don't have to marry just any farmer from Oregon…if you don't want to. I do care, Claire." He met her gaze once more. "I told you that. I don't lie."

But what did caring mean to him? Outside, lightning flashed, and a crack of thunder shook the windowpanes. The rain drummed even louder against the stable roof. She shivered.

"If it weren't for this stroke, I would have come back to marry you," he said, his voice low.

And she paused for a moment, digesting those words. He would have married her… and an image rose in her mind of the family they might have been—tall, strong Joel with those broad shoulders and bulky muscles. His laughter and fun, and that endearing protective streak of his… He would have made a fine father to Aaron, and a fine husband for her…

But he had had a stroke, and it had changed more than his body. It had changed his heart.

"There is no point in talking about what might have been," she said. "I've spent five years training myself to stop doing just that. It eats you up inside. It's better to look at life as it is—to face it."

Joel nodded. "I know. I've done that, too."

And yet, there was still that little image tucked away in her heart of that tall, strong husband who might have been hers.

"Let's get back inside," she said.

"Yah."

Claire led the way to the stable door. He'd said all sorts of sweet things five years ago, and she couldn't let herself be swayed by him again. Once he walked away from this property, there was no guarantee she'd ever see Joel again.

Chapter Three

Joel came out of the main-floor guest room into the warm, fragrant kitchen after changing into dry clothes. The bottom-floor guest suite, which included a bedroom and a sitting room, was an addition built onto the original house, normally called a dawdie hus, because it would have been used as an in-law suite. But for the purposes of the bed-and-breakfast, it worked beautifully.

The *Englisher* couple stood side by side in front of the side kitchen window, watching the rain come down. Joel had left his wet clothes hanging on a rack in front of the woodstove inside his room. He'd lit it with the kindling and wood that was provided for him, and his clothes would dry over the next few hours.

He pulled his door shut behind him just as Claire headed up the staircase, her wet dress clinging to her legs. She was only going to change now. She passed Aaron, who sat on the stairs, his dog next to him, looking bored.

"What's your dog's name?" Joel asked.

"I call him Goliath." Aaron scratched the dog's head. "But he's not mine."

"He sure looks like yours. He's always right at your side," Joel said.

"He's lost. My *mamm* saw a flyer his owners put up. We have to give him back after the storm."

Joel nodded. "I had a dog when I was your age."

"Yah?"

"His name was Puddle. Because he left lots of puddles everywhere." He shot the boy a grin.

Aaron's eyes lit up at the humor, and he laughed. "That's funny."

"Can I pet him?" Joel put a hand out, and the dog growled, the sound low and menacing. "Sorry, buddy," Joel said quietly. That dog did not like him, and he wasn't about to push it.

"I guess you can't." Aaron slid an arm

around the dog's neck. "I don't know why he does that."

"He wants to take care of you," Joel said. "It's okay. It's good to have a guardian like that."

Maybe *Gott* had sent a dog in Joel's absence, and that thought tugged at his heart.

"How come you walk funny?" Aaron asked.

"I had a stroke." He paused, wondering how to simplify that. "That means I got sick, and it affected my leg and arm."

"And your mouth a bit," Aaron said.

"Huh. I didn't know it was noticeable," Joel said with a half smile.

"It kind of is."

The honesty of children…

"How come you got sick?" Aaron asked.

"My *daet* got sick, too," Joel replied. "It's called a hereditary illness. It's just one of those things."

And it might affect his son, too, he realized. He swallowed, sending up a silent prayer—a little too late—that his ailment would never befall this child.

"Did your *daet* get well?" Aaron leaned forward.

"Well…" How much to tell a boy this small? "Um… Sort of like me, I guess."

His father had one arm that had virtually shriveled because he couldn't lift anything. He fell a lot. He kept trying to do chores, and when things went wrong, like he dropped a lit brand onto the kitchen floor, he blamed whatever child was closest. All the kids learned to stay clear of *Daet*, but they were wary, too. They knew enough to keep an eye on things to make sure the house didn't burn down. His father had had stroke after stroke, and the medicine didn't help as much as it should have. His doctors called him a "stubborn case."

"Oh, he was like you." Aaron looked sad. "That's not good. Sorry."

Did Joel look so bad? Sometimes he forgot what people saw when they looked at him. But this slim, lopsided version of himself would be the future.

"I saw you fall outside when you got off Old Jack," Aaron said. "I was watching at the window."

Joel froze. His son had seen that, too? His chest clenched, and all the things his *daet* used say in similar situations came flooding into his head.

You should have done it yourself! Lazy kids! What are you staring at? Get away from me! Get your mother in here. Tell her to quit dawdling around!

He'd hated his father most when he'd seen him at his weakest, because *Daet* was meanest then. And the fool man would never stop trying to keep doing the chores he used to do, even though he failed most of the time.

"*Yah*, I fell." Joel watched his son for a reaction.

Aaron squinted. "Did it hurt?"

"Um—" Not the question he'd expected. "*Yah*, a bit."

His hip ached still from how he'd landed. Some heat from the stove would help with that.

"Sorry." Aaron shrugged sympathetically. "I fell off the stairs, and I got a bad scrape. It's a scar now. You want to see?"

Without waiting for an answer, Aaron pulled up his pant leg and displayed a tear-shaped white scar on his knee. Joel leaned as close as Goliath would allow before the soft growl started again, and he nodded somberly.

"That probably hurt, too."

"*Yah.* I cried. And *Mamm* gave me a spoonful of sugar."

"Sugar?" he asked with a faint smile.

"When it hurts, she gives me sugar. She

said when the doctors gave me needles in the hospital when I was a little tiny baby, they gave me sugar to make it hurt less."

"That happened when you were born?" Joel asked.

"I think so."

Joel had missed so much. Why had Aaron needed needles? But this little man wouldn't know the answers to that. Claire was a good mother, he realized. Not that he'd questioned it, but it filled him with a quiet awe that she'd raised this child to this point on her own.

Claire came back down the stairs, now dressed in a dry, lilac-colored dress. She bent to ruffle Aaron's hair on her way by.

"Showing off your scar?" she asked.

Aaron smiled up at her and pulled his pant leg down. She brushed past him, smoothing a fresh white apron with her hands.

"We have an afternoon to while away," Claire said to the *Englishers*. "Would you like to do more basket weaving? Or perhaps read some books?"

"Do you have board games?" Gloria asked. "We haven't played one since the kids were young."

"It's been that long, hasn't it?" Ted looked

over at his wife. “Royden liked that Labyrinth game, remember?”

“He always beat us.” Gloria’s eyes misted, and she blinked back sudden tears. “Second thought, let’s do more basket weaving.”

Royden must be the son who passed away, Joel realized, and he looked down, trying to not stare at the very obvious grief on display.

“What about Dutch Blitz?” Aaron asked. “It’s fun!”

“Oh…” Ted started to shake his head.

“It’s not a board game,” Aaron said. “It’s got cards, and you’ve got to be really, really fast. I’m really good at it, but I’ll let you win, because it’s only polite.”

Aaron went over to stand at the kitchen table. He beamed at the *Englisher* couple hopefully, and Joel saw their reservations melt. Aaron was a hard boy to refuse, it seemed.

“Well, we could try,” Gloria said.

“I’ll go get it!” Aaron dashed up the stairs and a moment later came back down in a breathless flurry, a pack of cards in his hands. “I’ll show you how, okay?”

Aaron, Gloria and Ted put their attention into the card game, and Claire moved into the kitchen. She pulled a roasting pan out of a cupboard and a paper-wrapped piece of meat from the icebox. Joel limped over to where she was working.

"What happened when Aaron was born?"

"Hmm?" She looked up.

"He mentioned spoonsful of sugar when he's hurt, and how the doctors at the hospital did it for him, too."

"He was born early. They needed to do tests. And in the hospital, it wasn't a spoonful of sugar, it was a little bit of sucrose on the tip of a soother."

"How early was he born?" he asked.

"A few weeks. They said it was early labor brought on by stress."

Joel swallowed. "I'm sorry. It's my fault, I'm sure."

She didn't answer that, but she unwrapped the paper from around the meat—a pork shoulder—and pulled down some bottled seasonings.

"So what happened?" he prompted.

"He was born about three weeks early. He was over six pounds, though, and he was okay. But they did some tests. That's where the sugar came in, to distract him from the poke."

"That's...nice," he said.

"*Yah.*" She crossed her arms. "And it does work. I still do it. I don't know…a spoonful of sugar brings a smile back."

Joel nodded. "You're good at being a *mamm.*"

"I love him," she said simply. "That's all it takes—lots of love."

"When they did the blood tests," he said. "Um…they would have noticed if he had sickle cell anemia."

"They would have," she agreed. "But he didn't have any problems. He was perfectly healthy."

Joel out a slow breath. "Good…good. I'm glad. It's hereditary, you see."

"Oh…" Her eyes widened. "Oh!"

"If he doesn't have it, then we can thank *Gott* for that mercy," he said. "It's one less worry."

"*Yah*, that's true." Her gaze moved over to the table where Aaron was pointing out cards, and the *Englisher* couple looked very confused. Game instructions given by small children seldom made sense.

"How old is he?" he asked.

"He's almost five," she replied.

"He was born…in April?"

"March 29. He came early, remember?"

"Right." He let out a slow breath. "Right. Things a man should know about his son."

She looked at him mutely, and he could read the uncertainty in her gaze.

"Maybe we could find a way for me to send him birthday gifts, even if you're married," he said. "I could be...a friend? Maybe I could just be a distant relative. You could call me his uncle. Someone who cares. And when he's old enough, you could tell him more."

Claire pressed her lips together.

"I'm not trying to push you," he said. "I'm just realizing how much I missed."

Aaron as a baby, a toddler...learning to walk, to talk, to say *please* and *thank you*...

"I know. But you also promised not to say anything to him."

"And I won't," he insisted. "Not until you're ready. But Claire, he's my son, too."

"No!" Her eyes suddenly flashed up into anger, and she lowered her voice to a whisper. "No! He's not yours as much as he's mine! I carried him inside me, and then I gave birth to him with only my mother to hold my hand! I've raised him, taught him right from wrong, kissed his scrapes, made his food, sewed his clothes and worried and prayed over him! You have done none of that!"

He felt the strength of her anger in that whisper, and he almost took a step back.

"I didn't know about him," he said earnestly.

"You didn't. I understand that." Her hands shook, and she planted them on the counter. "But you don't get to walk in here and pretend that you have as much right to him as I do. Because you didn't come back, Joel."

Claire was right. In his effort to protect her from his illness, he'd abandoned her with their child. She sucked in a ragged breath, then reached for another bottle of seasoning.

Joel could tell that Claire felt threatened by him being here, and maybe he shouldn't blame her. He'd shown up just in time to ruin her chances at a marriage, after all she'd done on her own without his help or his support.

"If it weren't for the storm, you'd ask me to leave, wouldn't you?" he asked softly.

Claire looked up at him then, and her gaze hadn't softened. It was still like stone. "*Yah*, Joel. I would ask you to go."

"Then I thank *Gott* for springtime storms." He smiled. "I'm not your enemy, Claire. I'll show you that. Somehow."

"I don't have enemies," she said curtly.

"Good." He tried to catch her eye again, but she wouldn't look at him. The silence that stretched between them was taut, and he took a step back, wondering if there was anything else he could say.

Claire glanced up at him again and then looked toward the table.

"They might need clearer instructions over there," she said.

Getting rid of him. Right. "I can do that."

Joel limped over to the kitchen table and pulled out a chair.

"So…we start with how many cards?" Gloria asked feebly.

Joel looked over his shoulder toward Claire, who had turned toward the sink.

"First, we shuffle them really well," Joel said, reaching for the deck. "You mind if I explain it, Aaron?"

"Okay." Aaron shrugged. "They need extra help."

Joel exchanged a rueful smile with Ted and shuffled the deck. He'd find a way to show Claire that he wasn't here to make demands of her or make her life more difficult. There had to be a way for him to be in his son's life somehow…there had to be.

That evening, Claire looked out the bedroom window, rain still pattering against the pane.

The sun had set, and outside was the kind of inky darkness that blocked out their view of much beyond their own reflection in the window, but when she shaded her eyes and leaned close to the glass, she could see water collecting on the driveway. The house and stable were on the highest ground, though, and all she could do was pray that the rain would stop soon.

Claire left the window and sat down on the edge of her son's bed. She tapped Aaron's nose with the tip of her finger and smiled. His blond curls shone in the low light of the kerosene lamp on the bedside table next to him.

"I'm going to need your help tomorrow," Claire said. "We have three unexpected guests. That's a lot of work."

These days when she got extra guests, she'd been calling on her friend Sarai to come help her with the cooking and laundry when Sarai wasn't busy with her grandmother's house and their egg business. But Sarai might as well be across the county in a storm like this.

"*Yah*, I can help," Aaron said, and he rolled over in his bed. Claire tugged his quilt higher up on his shoulders. "I'm a good helper."

Claire could hear the Wassels in the bedroom next door, their voices soft as they talked to each other. At least she kept the guest rooms clean and the beds made. Her mother had always told her that procrastinating only gave today's work to tomorrow, and sometimes surprises came. It was a lesson that had stuck.

"You are a good helper, Aaron," she said. "Let's say your prayer."

Aaron shut his eyes tightly.

"Dear *Gott*, take care of us as we sleep, and wake us tomorrow, happy and ready to do Your will," she prayed.

"Amen." Aaron's eyes popped open. "Tomorrow, can I go see the tree over the road?"

"We'll go look at it if the rain stops." Outside, the wind whipped pellets of rain against the side of the house as if in response.

"*Will* the rain stop?" Aaron asked.

"Eventually. It can't rain forever."

"Will the water reach the house?"

"I doubt it." At least she hoped not. "We have friends who will come help us if it gets worse. Don't you worry. But the rain will stop eventually. My father, your *dawdie*, always told me that storms pass—they have to pass. They run out of wind and rain and lightning, and we get sunshine again. So always remember that, Aaron. Storms always pass."

Her father had told her that when she'd been pregnant with Aaron, too. He'd told her that when she was a young mother with an infant and no husband. He'd told her that when Aaron was teething and she was exhausted and when Aaron was a toddler and kept running out the door every chance he got. Storms passed. Clouds ran out of rain, and children grew out of their phases. Even gossip lost its power over time.

And wasn't Claire a walking example of just that? On her bedroom dresser there was that letter from Adam Lantz from Oregon to answer. An honest marriage possibility. And somehow, she still hadn't picked up a pen and paper to reply.

"I hope the storm stops soon, because I want to see the fallen tree," her son said.

"*Yah, yah,*" she said. "I know. We'll have to wait, though."

"Can we play chutes and ladders with the guests?" Aaron asked.

"That's a question for tomorrow. You go to sleep now," Claire said. "Morning will be here soon enough."

"Will Joel help you with the horses?" Aaron ignored her attempt to end the conversation.

"I imagine he will," she said. "Men help with outdoor work. It's how things go."

"But he fell down, *Mamm.*" Aaron looked

up at her worriedly. "You saw it, right? He fell right down, and it hurt his backside."

Claire nodded. "*Yah.* I saw that. But I think it would offend him if a woman took care of things out there where men are supposed to do the work."

"I could do it," Aaron said. "I'll take care of the horses."

"You're a little boy."

"But I could do it!"

Claire put a hand on Aaron's cheek. "You're a good boy, Aaron. But that's work for grown-ups and older kids. When you're old enough, I'll send you to care for the horses, okay?"

Aaron sighed. "Okay."

"Time for sleep."

"Night-night."

She bent and kissed his forehead. "Night-night."

Claire closed her son's door behind her, and the door to the guest room opened then. Gloria was still dressed in her regular clothes, even though Claire had lent her a nightgown.

"You have a very good selection of Christian novels." Gloria lifted a book up as proof. "If it's okay with you, Ted and I thought we'd just read the evening away. I can't tell you how nice it is to be away from Wi-Fi and the TV."

"Of course." Claire smiled. "Enjoy. Come down and eat if you get hungry, too. I'm stocked up with fresh muffins and pastries. There is even half a shoofly pie, if you'd like to try it."

"Maybe later," Gloria said. "But thank you so much for your hospitality."

"It's nothing." Claire exchanged a smile with the older woman, then carried on down the stairs.

The kitchen was empty, and she paused by the counter, watching the rain lash the glass of the window over the sink. The storm hadn't let up—the torrents that kept coming down were worrying, and she shaded her eyes to get a better look out the window as she had upstairs, but she couldn't make out much more. Just rain and more rain.

Claire heard the door open, and she looked over to see Joel come into the kitchen from the guest suite. He headed for the wood box beside the door.

"I can bring you some wood," she said. "I'm sorry, I thought there was enough in that room. That's my fault."

"I can get it." He waved her off. "I was drying my clothes, so I stoked it up."

She nodded.

"You're in hostess mode," he said.

"It's my job."

Joel met her gaze. "Don't do that with me, okay? I'm not an *Englisher* here for an Amish experience. You don't need to put chocolates on my pillow or cater to my needs."

The chocolate...it hadn't been for him specifically.

"I...put chocolates on all the pillows."

He smiled, then, and she could almost see the old Joel in that smile.

"I did like the chocolate," he admitted. "But I'm saying that I want to make your life easier, not harder."

Joel picked up an armload of wood and limped back in the direction of the guest room.

"How did you find me?" she asked as he reached the door.

He turned back. "I told you. I asked around."

"Why did you even start looking?" she asked. "It had been five years. You didn't know about our son. Why did you even bother?"

Joel leaned against the doorjamb. "Because my father died."

"How does that have anything to do with me?"

"I realized I was relieved he was gone."

She blinked. "What?"

"That sounds awful." He adjusted the wood in his good arm. "I know it. That relief was mingled with grief, too. Don't get me wrong—I did love my *daet*, but he was a hard man to get along with. The sicker he got, the harder he was to like. He lashed out at us kids when we were growing up. It's why I started traveling to different states, working in different areas. I wanted to get as far from home as I could. When he finally passed six months ago…" He sighed. "When he finally passed away, I realized that for all the time I spent avoiding him, I'm a lot like him, too."

Claire stayed silent, and Joel straightened. "I started looking for you because I wanted to know what became of you. Maybe I wanted to see you married with three *kinner* and a houseful of in-laws so I could feel better about how I left things with you. Leaving, not ever coming back—that was my biggest regret."

She held her breath.

"I should have explained, sent a letter, something," he said. "But I was a coward."

"Oh…" That was what he meant.

"But I should be clear," he said softly. "I'm not here to ruin your chances at marriage with another man. I know what's waiting for me with this illness, if I'm anything like my father."

"You think you'll end up like your *daet*?"

"I know I will. I have the same illness, and now that I'm struggling with a body that won't listen to me like it used to, I'm understanding his anger about it a whole lot more."

"You don't have to be bitter like he was," she said.

Joel shrugged, then nodded. "I know. Attitude matters and all that." He licked his lips. "But Aaron saw me fall. Did you know that?"

"Yah."

"Do you know what I felt when Aaron told me he'd seen that?" Joel asked.

She shook her head.

"Shame. I was ashamed he'd seen his father on the ground like that. And shame is a powerful acid." He sighed. "I saw exactly what it did to my father. Don't worry, Claire. I have no intention of inflicting myself with this illness on you for any length of time. You'll have your life, and you will have more than you started out with. I'll make sure of it. But I'm not going to let Aaron grow up seeing me decline. I won't have him pity me, or worse, resent me for dragging you down, too."

Claire let out a slow, shaky breath.

"I won't be your problem, Claire." Joel adjusted the wood in his arms once more and opened his door. "Good night."

His limping footsteps faded into the guest suite.

Joel didn't intend to stay. He'd come to give her his inheritance and leave. Claire should be relieved. It was an almost unheard-of gift… except, even though he insisted that his future wouldn't be her worry, she couldn't help but wonder who would take care of Joel if his health got worse and he had no inheritance to support him. Who would make sure he ate? Who would make him comfortable?

But Joel hadn't come back for her, and that was an important detail. And there was a farmer willing to write letters with her. Maybe she should see that letter as a gift instead of being afraid of all the possibilities. Adam Lantz could be perfectly kind. Maybe he'd be generous and indulgent of a new stepson.

Outside that kitchen window, the rain continued to fall.

Gott, she prayed, *I wish Joel hadn't come back. It would be easier then.*

Because now, even when Joel left again,

she couldn't go on resenting the callous liar who'd gotten her pregnant. He hadn't known about his son, and when he learned that he might be a father, he came with an offer of financial support. He'd done the right thing. He wasn't a bad man, after all. And that robbed her of a very comfortable story.

Now, she couldn't say she was an abandoned woman who'd been treated unfairly. She'd just be a woman who'd never been enough. And that was worse.

Chapter Four

The next morning, Claire woke up early to do chores, as she always did. Her bedroom was cold, and she shivered as she pulled on her dress and added a thick, knitted cardigan on top. She left Aaron sleeping in his little bed, adding one more blanket on top of him before she crept downstairs, hoping not to disturb her guests. She kindled a fire in the woodstove in the kitchen and added wood until it held a nice, cheery glow and held her hands out toward the welcome warmth. Outside, the wind howled and rattled down the stovepipe.

She hadn't slept well the night before. Joel had been right downstairs…right there! For years, she'd longed for a chance like this one—a chance to talk to him face-to-face and to ask him why he'd left like that. And now she had her chance, and he was here offering explanations and financial support... and it was picking open old wounds that she'd thought were healed.

She hadn't felt sad last night in her bed. She'd felt furious! Joel had left, gotten sick, never sent word to her, never told her why he did what he did. Just left. And while her faith told her that she needed to forgive him, all the old anger was back in a flood. It had taken hours to fall asleep, and she awoke at her usual hour exhausted.

Claire adjusted a vent to let the wood burn more slowly, and as she slid the heavy vent to the side, the door to the guest suite opened, and Joel appeared in the doorway. He was dressed, and he'd shaved, too.

"Sorry to disturb you," she said, but her voice was tight.

"I'm up and dressed," he replied. "I'll help you with chores."

"I can do it."

"I said I'd help." He eyed her. "You're angry again."

"Joel, I'm angry still." She shook her head. "I'm sorry. I tried to do the Christian thing and let it all go, but it came back."

Joel nodded. "I probably deserve that."

Claire turned toward the mudroom, and Joel followed. She put on her coat over her cardigan and stepped into her rubber boots. Joel grabbed his coat and hat off a peg.

"I'm glad to see you still make those beautiful baskets." He nodded up to the baskets lining a shelf that held everything from mittens and hats to ice skates and flashlights. They were some of her more meticulous work, put to good use. That was how Claire liked to do things—create something beautiful and then put it to work.

"I've always liked weaving."

"I know. You tried to teach me, remember?"

Her mind went back to that summer when she'd put her hands over his, trying to guide him in the work. He'd had big, farmer's hands—callused, strong and not very suited to delicate work.

"You weren't very good at it." She smiled.

"But you were." He smiled back. "Claire, the whole time I was in the hospital, I kept remembering every second of that summer together. It was the best time of my life."

"And that memory was packaged up and set aside," she said. "The best things in life last, Joel."

He nodded. "I know. I just wanted you to understand—"

She put a hand against his chest—something she used to do back when they'd been in love—and then she pulled her hand down quickly when she realized what she'd done.

"Joel, I don't want to know what you felt for me back then," she said, her voice tight. "If you thought you loved me, if you remembered our time together fondly…it doesn't matter one bit. I'm sorry, but it doesn't. You left. I'm here raising our son on my own. That's the life I have, and what you felt then, or what you feel now, doesn't change that, does it?"

Joel was silent, and she met his gaze evenly. She was surprised she was able to, considering the tumult of emotion flooding through her, but looking at him now, some of the power of those memories had dissipated. He was no longer the strapping young man who'd made her melt at a look. He was older, thinner, more worn, and while she felt that old yearning toward him, time had passed. This heartbreak wasn't fresh. She now knew how to carry it.

Claire didn't wait for him to answer her—she just opened the door and plunged out into the rain. Joel might have come to find her at long last, but she was no longer the naive, lovestruck young woman she used to be. She was now someone's mother—and that had changed a whole lot more than Joel probably imagined.

After chores were complete, Joel headed upstairs to shower. Claire opened up the damper on the stove again, added more split wood, and then got ready to start breakfast. Aaron came downstairs with his wooden farm set.

"Can I play cows?" Aaron asked. That was what he called his little game where he set up his farm and arranged his wooden cattle all over the floor to "graze."

"*Yah*, but go play in the sitting room," she replied. "We have a full house today."

"Okay." Aaron carried his set off toward the other room, and she could hear the thump and clatter of the toys on the hardwood floor. She smiled at the sound of his game and turned back to the work at hand.

She'd make oatmeal this morning with raisins in it and some corn bread on the side. She had some jarred applesauce that went well on top of corn bread, and that should fill everyone up and keep them warm in this chilly downpour.

"Can I help you with anything in the kitchen?"

Claire turned to see Gloria at the bottom of the stairs. She was dressed in her clothes from yesterday. With a quick perusal of the woman's garments—woolen pants, a very soft-looking sweater with some beading on it—Claire didn't think she'd be able to safely wash any of it.

"Of course," Claire said. "I can lend you some of my clothes while you're here, if you like."

"That would be nice. Maybe for tomorrow. I can wear these for today." Gloria accepted an apron from Claire and put it on. "My husband is still sleeping. I thought I'd just let him rest. At home he tends to sleep in. That's a perk of being retired."

That wasn't a perk that the Amish enjoyed. There was work to do at any age. But their ways were different, and she could appreciate an older man being tired out.

"Definitely let him sleep," Claire replied. "Were you comfortable?"

"Very," Gloria said. "I haven't slept that

well in years. There's something about rain falling outside that is so comforting."

"*Yah.* For farmers, too," Claire agreed. "A lengthy rain is good for crops, but this much…"

Claire looked toward the gray window, where raindrops were still pouring down the glass. This much would flood the area and wash away topsoil, too. At least it was early enough in the year that nothing had been planted yet.

"Do you come from a farming family?" Gloria asked.

"*Yah.* Out in Ohio."

"My husband was raised on a farm," Gloria said. "He has all sorts of stories about runaway hogs and horses with attitude."

Claire chuckled. "The best way to grow up."

"Hmm." Gloria's smile evaporated. "We raised our kids in town. I used to think that farms were dangerous for kids. You hear of accidents happening, you know?"

Gloria looked over at her, and Claire could see the vulnerability in the woman's face. She wanted to be understood.

"*Yah, mamms* worry," Claire said softly. "I worry plenty, too."

"We do." Gloria nodded. "Maybe too much. Or about the wrong things. My oldest son, Royden, died three years ago."

"Oh..." Claire turned toward the other woman. "I'm so sorry. What happened?"

"It was a boating accident." Gloria blinked back some tears. "I'm sorry. Yesterday was the anniversary of his death. We wanted to do something else—distract ourselves. But the very next day, the sadness is still there. You can't run from it, can you?"

If it weren't for this storm, Gloria would be at home right now, with her memories, and her husband...and her privacy. But maybe *Gott* had wanted her here for her tough day after the anniversary.

Claire reached over and gave Gloria's hand a squeeze. "I daresay you can't."

She had her own griefs that she hadn't been able to put into the past, either, but Gloria's was worse. Much worse.

Gloria sucked in a deep breath. "We got past Christmas. That's the hardest holiday without Royden. We have so many happy Christmas memories with him, and now..." Gloria smiled faintly. "Can I tell you something?"

"*Yah*, of course."

"When Royden was little, the Christmas

story was about a baby being born and beautiful possibilities. We raised him knowing that Santa wasn't real, but we played along with the game anyway, you know?"

Claire didn't really know. The Amish didn't entertain Santa in their homes, but now wasn't the time to say that. "The *kinner* do love Christmas."

"*Kinner.* That's children?"

"*Yah.* Sorry. I mix languages sometimes."

"No worries," Gloria said. "I like it. You have a beautiful language. Anyway, I know some mothers who've lost children avoid Christmas altogether because the happy memories of their child's early Christmases just tear their hearts out. But as Christians, Christmas isn't about Santa—not really. It's about Jesus coming to earth in the form of a helpless baby and saving us from all this sadness and heartbreak."

"Amen," Claire murmured.

"So while Royden was little, I identified with Mary as a young mother. And now I identify with Mary at the cross—losing her son, watching him die…"

Claire's eyes misted, and her throat tightened.

"That first Christmas after burying Royden, we went to the Christmas Eve service at our church, and I just sobbed my heart out."

"Because you missed him," Claire whispered.

"Yes, but more than that," Gloria said softly. "I was so heart-wrenchingly grateful that Jesus had come down at all, that he'd given us a way to Heaven so that I had the hope of seeing my beautiful boy again. Christmas became less of a twinkly celebration and more of a life raft."

Claire nodded. "I can understand that."

"Easter has a deeper meaning now, too," Gloria went on. "It's coming up next month, and you know what? I'm not going to be joyful because He has risen. I'm probably going to cry my heart out all over again, because Jesus came to rescue heartbroken mothers with empty arms. Every Christian holiday seems to be the same for me now. The happy, bright, shiny enjoyment is gone, and in its place is this deep gratefulness that God has given us an escape route from the pain." Gloria looked over at Claire, then away, seemingly embarrassed. "That probably doesn't make sense to someone as young as you."

"It makes more sense than you think," Claire said. "My life hasn't been easy."

"Did you lose your husband?"

Claire felt her cheeks heat. She was asked this question often. "Not in the way you're thinking. Aaron's dad…left me."

"Oh." Gloria nodded sympathetically. "I'm really sorry."

"It's okay. I'm doing all right."

"I've heard that kind of loss can be even more painful than a death," Gloria said gently. "So you know, then."

Claire nodded. *Yah*, she knew about pain, and she'd waded through her own grief and heartbreak. It wasn't like losing a child, but she'd lost the man she thought she'd marry… and he'd torn out a piece of her heart that she'd never gotten back.

"If I were to give you any advice," Gloria said, then stopped. "If you wanted to hear it, that is…"

"I do want to hear it."

"Then I would tell you to enjoy these holidays with your little boy. Let this Easter be about family gatherings and a big meal and baby animals… Let Christmases be about children opening presents and about Jesus being born and happy carols. Don't feel bad for one moment about enjoying that level of things," Gloria said. "This time when they're little is oh so short. But also know that when life moves on and if, God forbid, something should happen to break your heart again, you can also know that those very holidays that held so much joy in these early years have a depth of comfort waiting for you when you need it most."

Claire held the older woman's gaze, and she felt a sense of peace settle into her heart along with the woman's words. "That's…very wise."

"My dear," Gloria said with a motherly smile. "That's just life experience talking."

Claire smiled then, and she felt a wave of gratefulness for this storm that had locked an *Englisher* couple in with her. She'd thought perhaps *Gott* wanted to use her to comfort Gloria, but it looked like Gloria had something to offer, too.

"Shall we cook?" Claire reached for a pot to make the oatmeal. "If you want to go grab a bowl over there, I've got a corn bread recipe you can start on."

Yah, it was true. *Gott* certainly did work in unexpected ways.

The day was a long one for Joel, with everyone being cooped up inside and the rain pouring down the windows. There wasn't much to do besides sit with a book or play a game of chutes and ladders with Aaron… and Aaron cheated. The little boy counted his moves with heart more than with his head, and he always ended up on top.

"I win!" Aaron called out cheerily. "I'm very good at this game."

"*Yah*, apparently." Joel chuckled. "Very good. Are you this good when you play with other *kinner*?"

"I don't have other *kinner* to play it with. But I always win with grown-ups."

Ted and Gloria sat at the other end of the kitchen table, working on baskets again. They murmured together as they worked, Gloria seeming to have more natural talent for the craft than her husband did, but Joel was rather impressed with the man's dogged determination.

Goliath padded over to the water dish, and Claire came over to the table and looked over her son's shoulder. Then she raised her gaze to meet Joel's meaningfully.

"Don't let him do that," Claire told him quietly. "He needs to learn to count properly."

She tapped Aaron's shoulder. "Count properly, son."

She headed back into the depths of the kitchen, a few yards from the kitchen table, where she was baking bread. She pulled dough out of a bowl and started to knead it on a floured counter, leaning into the dough with all her weight.

Joel turned his attention back to the game, and Aaron spun the dial. He moved his little paper boy across the board, skimming over the squares and counting merrily—and inaccurately—as he went. Joel didn't have the heart to make him stop and count. He was half-afraid that Aaron would lose interest in playing with him.

"My turn," Joel said. This time, he'd decided on a new tactic. He spun the dial, and he did exactly as Aaron had—he started counting with his heart, too, whipping across the board, sliding down chute after chute.

"Wait…" Aaron stopped him, putting his small hand over his. "I think you're doing it wrong."

"Nope," Joel said. "I thought that was how we were playing."

Aaron was thoughtful for a moment, his little mouth pressed together in a thin line.

"Aaron," Claire called, flipping the dough

over and leaning into it once more, "are you being honest in your game?"

The word *honest* brought this to a new level, and Aaron didn't answer, but his lips stayed tightly shut. Then he spun the dial and picked up his playing piece.

"One…two…three…four…five…seven."

"Six…" Joel said softly.

"Six," Aaron said. "Now seven?"

Joel nodded.

"Seven." He stopped at the right place. "Your turn."

Joel spun and made his own move, and when he glanced over at the *Englisher* couple, he found Ted watching him with an approving look on his face. Then he turned his attention back to the basket in front of him.

Maybe Joel was doing something right. One thing he knew was that *daets* dealt with issues differently than *mamms* did. His own *daet* had left him frustrated and angry in his youth, but he'd seen other fathers and sons on the men's side of worship services. And only now that he knew about Aaron was he starting to wonder how he would do this… how he would be an influence in Aaron's life that was better than the one his father had been for him.

But Claire didn't seem open to that. She had plans of her own—ones he'd never ask her to sacrifice—but looking at her kneading that dough, and his son flicking the spinner, he felt a tug toward them.

The rest of the day slipped away with a few more games, some reading in the sitting room and a nap when he nodded off with a copy of *The Budget* on his lap. Lunch was eaten, the dog was let outside to do his business and then dinner was served. He'd offered to help Claire with cleanup, but she'd refused.

"You're a guest here," she said pointedly.

Yah, a guest. And no one was to know otherwise. So he'd gone out to the stable, brushed down some horses and had some time alone in the comfortable, warm enclosure before cleaning out the stalls a little bit early.

When he came back inside, Claire was just putting on her boots.

"The chores are done," he said, his voice low.

"*Yah?*" She smiled faintly. "I'd argue that you should have at least let me help, but I've been very busy inside, and it's kind of you. Thank you, Joel."

The earlier testiness seemed to be gone, and in its place was tiredness. She stepped back out of her boots and into her house shoes, bending down to pull them over her heels.

"*Yah.* Not a problem," he said.

"It's time to put Aaron to bed," she said, and then she paused. "Um… I normally read him a Bible story."

"Yah?"

"Maybe you'd like to read it tonight?"

She was offering something rather special, and he nodded quickly. "*Yah*, I could do that."

"Okay, then." She brushed past him, heading back out of the mudroom, and he let out a slow breath. The soft scent of baked bread lingered in the air, and for just a moment, he wondered if this was what it would feel like to have his own family, and it was like the careful wall around his heart had suddenly sprung a leak. But he pushed back the unbidden longing. He knew better—his own mother had gone through more than any woman should with his father's illness. He wouldn't impose himself on Claire like that.

But tonight, he could read his son a story.

When he went inside, the *Englisher* couple were nowhere to be seen, but the dog was stretched out in front of the woodstove, enjoying the warmth. Joel glanced around, and Claire seemed to notice his curiosity.

"The Wassels went to read upstairs," she said. "I guess they need some personal space, too."

And he needed some time alone with Claire and Aaron, so it worked out rather well. Aaron was in blue pajamas, his feet bare and his curly hair rumpled, and he squatted next to the dog, petting him.

"Aaron, Joel is going to read the story tonight," Claire said.

"*Yah?*" Aaron looked over, obviously surprised. "How come?"

"He wants to," she said. "Go to the couch, son."

Aaron headed off toward the sitting room, the dog following him, and Joel looked down at Claire.

"What do I read him?" he asked.

"Whatever you want to," she replied.

If she meant that to be helpful, it wasn't. But at least she was giving him a choice. They followed Aaron together, and Aaron plopped himself into the center of the couch so that there was space on either side of him. Joel looked over at Claire, and he saw some pink in her cheeks. This was feeling decidedly domestic all of a sudden.

"Go lie down," Claire said to the dog in

English, and the dog went to the center of the rag rug in the middle of the room and flopped down.

Joel cleared his throat and sat down on one side of Aaron, and Claire slid in on the other side, her knees pressed together. She passed a heavy Bible over to Joel, and his pulse sped up.

Gott, guide me, he prayed silently.

He opened the Bible, he dropped his gaze down to the page. It was the book of 1 Samuel, and the story was a familiar one—the anointing of David when he was just a shepherd boy. This was it—the right story for a little boy learning that his actions mattered, even now.

So Joel read the story—how David's big brothers were all considered by the prophet first, and how the prophet thought surely it would be them whom *Gott* had chosen. Then the prophet worked his way through all the brothers until he got to the youngest brother, David, who worked out in the fields with the sheep. He was the one chosen to be king, to everyone's surprise.

"Do you know why *Gott* chose David?" Joel asked Aaron.

Aaron shook his head.

"Because even in his work with the sheep, David did the right thing and followed *Gott*'s ways," Joel said. "It's a good lesson for boys. Even when you help your *mamm* in the house, when you feed your dog or when you play a game, all of your choices are important. Even now."

Aaron squirmed a little bit. "Okay. Are we done?"

The boy was almost five, but he'd have to hear this story a hundred more times before it would land in just the right way…probably when he was a young teenager. That was how "raising a child in the way he should go" worked—repetition, consistency and the Bible. At least that was what the bishop in Joel's home community had been saying in his sermons lately…sermons that seemed to be very well-timed, considering Joel's recent discovery.

Claire took Aaron up to bed for his prayers, and Joel stayed respectfully downstairs. He might be Aaron's father, but he wasn't the one raising him. This was Claire's domain.

Joel put the Bible on the table next to the couch and rubbed his hands over his face. If *Gott* chose the worthy among them because of their goodness and obedience, the likes of Joel were in trouble. Because he'd known right from wrong. He'd known better. But a few chapters later, in that same book of the Bible, there were more stories about David—stories where David made very big, very shameful mistakes. And that was the point in his life where Joel found himself now.

Joel had to make up for what he'd done to Claire, and somehow just handing the money from his inheritance over to her didn't seem like quite enough. Not anymore.

Chapter Five

As Claire came back down the stairs, she could hear the Wassels' voices as they talked together in their room. It seemed like a pleasant enough conversation, because Gloria's laugh suddenly rang out, and Ted's deeper voice chuckled along with her. Then they stopped, and their tones turned more melancholy.

This was a hard time for the couple, Claire now knew, but they were still finding joy, laughter and connection. It was admirable. Working at this bed-and-breakfast, Claire had witnessed many couples. Some were tense and working through some issues with a weekend away. Some were quiet and stable. Others were newly married, and one couple that stood out had come for a trip, just the two of them, but had left their young children behind, and the wife was worrying more than enjoying the break. Claire could understand that sentiment, since she'd never been away from her own son yet. Watching the way different couples related to each other intrigued her.

When she was a teenager, she and her sisters used to watch young Amish people from other communities when they went visiting and try to guess which ones were secretly engaged, which were courting, which were just getting to know each other, all by their body language. Back then, she'd hoped to be engaged, then married herself. But life held some bitter ironies.

All the same, the Wassels' relationship seemed special—not only in their length of marriage, but also in their ability to pull together during hard times instead of pushing apart.

As Claire came down the stairs, these thoughts milling through her mind, she heard water running, and she emerged into the kitchen to see Joel with his back to her, filling a sink with sudsy water.

"Joel?"

He turned, gave her a nod and then turned his back again.

"Joel, you're supposed to be a guest here," she reminded him.

"I can pitch in."

"It will look…suspicious."

He looked over his shoulder again. "To whom? Your guests? I doubt they care what sort of relationship is between us. And as for Aaron…he's too young to notice."

"Not too young to talk about it later." She leaned against the side of the counter.

Joel shrugged. "I read him his Bible story. That's more suspicious than me helping you with dishes."

Yah, she'd slipped there. She shouldn't have done that, but she'd wanted to give Joel something from his time with his son, and she'd noticed how well he'd gotten Aaron to start playing chutes and ladders by the rules. He'd done it differently than she would have, but it had worked.

"Fine," Claire relented. "If you really want to wash dishes—"

"I do." He gave her a level look and turned back to the sink.

Stubborn. Back when she'd fallen for him, she'd thought he was strong, and that determined attitude had made her heart flutter. Now? He was just plain stubborn.

Claire picked up a dish towel, and when he rinsed a plate, she took it from the draining board and dried it.

"Alone at last." He glanced down at her.

Back when he'd take her walking, he'd hold her hand and tug her in close against him and murmur those very words as if it were a crushing relief just to get her off where no one else could interrupt, and they'd just stroll along, hand in hand. Claire swallowed, pushing back the sweet memory.

"We've been surrounded by people all day," he added.

"I normally use cleaning up the kitchen in the evening as my alone time. I can think and pray and… I don't know, just get my balance back after a busy day."

"I get enough time on my own," he said. "It's not a luxury for me. It's…more of a burden."

He was lonely. She didn't know why that should surprise her.

"Do you live alone?" Claire asked.

"I live with my *mamm*."

"You should court someone." He didn't answer, and she sighed. She got that advice all the time. Just get married! "Not always so simple, I know."

"I won't get married," he said.

"What?" She squinted up at him. "I mean, eventually..."

"No."

"Ever?"

He shook his head. "I'm not doing it. I know what this illness looks like. I know what it does—at least in our family. Before my *daet* passed away, I always thought my *mamm* was the strongest woman I knew. When *Daet* was driving the rest of us around the bend with his complaining and barking, *Mamm* would just sweetly bring him something to eat, or a cup of tea, and nothing seemed to get to her. But then one day, *Daet* dropped something on his foot, and he got furious. He was yelling and blaming it on *Mamm* for some silly reason, and instead of being patient and sweet like she always was, *Mamm* just walked out the door." Joel put another dish in the rack and pulled a few more into the soapy water. "I mean, she just walked out. She put on her shoes, and she walked out the door and just kept walking. Me and my brothers stood there and watched her go from the doorway."

"Where did she go?" Claire asked.

"Up the drive, and... I don't know. I didn't

follow her. I thought she'd come back, but it took two days for her to return."

Claire gasped. "Two days!"

"We were frantic. We looked everywhere. We asked around at the homes of friends and family, and…nothing. She was just gone."

"But she did come back," Claire prompted.

"*Yah.* She came back two days later in a taxi. She got out, took money out of the cookie tin, paid her fare and never spoke of it again."

"No explanation?" Claire asked.

Claire could possibly understand a woman getting to the end of her patience and saying something sharp, or to the end of her endurance and taking a walk, but wouldn't she come back feeling terrible about leaving her family like that after two days?

"No explanation was needed, really," Joel replied.

"You weren't upset?" Claire pressed.

"I was worried about her."

"But not angry she'd abandoned you all like that?"

"I was a grown man. I was capable of taking care of myself. It wasn't like I was a little boy," he said. "Besides, I understood her getting to the end of her endurance with him. My *daet* was really hard to deal with. *Mamm* was sweet and calm until she just couldn't take *Daet*'s bitterness anymore. *Daet* was more careful after that, too, but *Mamm* was never quite the same, either."

"How was she different?" Claire asked.

"She did her duty—she cooked and cleaned—but she was tougher after that. She didn't take as much guff—from any of us!"

"And your *daet*?"

"He was furious with her," Joel replied. "But I think he knew he had it coming, after all those years of being so ornery. So he did his best to be nicer, to bite his tongue more often—at least with her. But it never really fixed things. He had a massive stroke and died about a year later."

Claire was silent. She'd never heard of an Amish wife doing such a thing before. Mind you, if any of them did walk away for a few days at a time, it would be shocking enough to hide. But still... She picked up another plate to dry.

"I don't want to be the man who drives a woman to walk away like that," Joel said. "And I understand my *daet*'s anger and frustration. I feel it, too, when I fall down, or drop things, or trip over the ground I'm walking on because I can't get my leg to lift far enough… It's the most frustrating thing, and I'm not going to get married and put a woman through the life my *mamm* had. She didn't know what life with him would be like. I do know what life with me might turn into, and I won't do it."

"You really think you'd be like him?" Claire paused with a dish in her hand and looked up at him.

"I might." He rinsed another plate and put it in the rack. "I wouldn't want to, and I'd try not to, but… I might. That's what scares me. So I won't even start a romantic relationship. Besides, a woman needs a man who can physically take care of things. That's not me anymore."

They were silent for a minute or two as they continued with the dishes. Claire put a stack of plates away, and Joel started on the cups and cutlery. Somehow, it felt nice to have someone to talk to. Joel might not be her answer anymore, but his life hadn't been perfect, either, and there was balm in that shared sense of life's difficulties.

"Well, I have my own reasons for being cautious," Claire said after a bit. "I said I'd never have an arranged marriage, but then

Naomi, my friend who used to run this bed-and-breakfast, got married and moved away with her husband, and I… I don't know. I suppose I got lonely."

"You thought you'd stay two spinsters together?" he asked with a faint smile.

"*Yah.*" But she wasn't joking. She'd really had a sweet image in her mind of two good friends who could run a business together and support each other as they grew older. She had more friends in the community, like Sarai, but Sarai wouldn't stay single long. She was beautiful, funny, full of personality. She'd find the man she wanted soon enough.

"I was teasing," Joel said. "I doubt you'll stay single."

"Then you don't know how hard it is to find a husband when you have a child already."

"Plenty of widows do it."

"I'm not a widow, though, am I?"

Joel nodded, and she saw his jaw clench. "So you changed your mind and went to the matchmaker?"

"I did. I'm embarrassed about that now."

"Embarrassed?" Joel looked down at her, his dark gaze meeting hers. "There's no shame in wanting love, Claire."

"I suppose I wanted to find it the regular

way, with a man coming to call on me, and…" And taking her home from singing. But that was how young people met, not women with children of their own. She didn't finish the thought. Instead, she picked up the next dish.

"Sometimes life is different than we expect," Joel said. "But it can still be beautiful."

"Says the man who won't ever marry," she said with a rueful smile.

"I have an idea."

She looked up at him warily. "What's that?"

"I know we thought we'd be more to each other when we first met. But what if we…" He swallowed. "What if we were friends, Claire?"

"Friends?" She squinted up at him.

"*Yah.*" He put more energy into the washing of dishes and rinsed off three more cups before he continued. "What if we could be there for each other as friends? What if I could help you with Aaron as he grows up, and you could help me with…oh, I don't know, just keeping me company some? We loved each other once. Maybe we could turn that into something different but still beautiful."

Claire let out a slow breath. "But your home is in Indiana."

"I could move out here. I'm sure I can find some clients to do bookkeeping. It's in demand, you know." He looked down at her. "Taking that bookkeeping class was a good choice."

Joel pulled his hands from the water and reached for the towel in her hands. His wet fingers caught hers, along with the towel, and they both froze.

Claire dropped her gaze, and those hands—they were the same still. They weren't quite so strong, but she'd memorized his fingers, his knuckles, the breadth of his palms…

"I think that would be hard for me," she whispered.

"I wouldn't ask for more."

And that was hard part she was embarrassed to admit. Joel wouldn't ask for more from her. He wanted to be her friend, to help her with her son, but not to have her heart. That would hurt every single day.

"Joel, I—" She raised her eyes, and her words caught in her throat. His agonized gaze was locked on her face, and his fingers closed gently over hers. "I don't think I could do that."

Joel let go of her fingers and turned back to the sink. "I understand."

"Do you, though?" Claire pressed.

"I'm hard to forgive."

"I *loved* you! I know I've been angry

since you came back, but this isn't about my anger. I really, deeply loved you. And maybe I should have held my heart back a little bit. I know we overstepped in other ways in our relationship, but maybe I should have been more cautious with my heart, too, until after some wedding vows."

Joel stopped washing, and she saw his shoulders rise and fall with a shaky breath.

"Me, too."

"We were young and stupid," she said.

"Maybe."

Joel rinsed another mug and set it in the rack. It was strange to watch a man doing her dishes as if he belonged here somehow. But Joel did *not* belong here. He belonged back in Indiana with his family, or maybe for her he just belonged in the past in her memories. He didn't belong out here in Redemption with her fresh start.

"What do you mean, maybe?" She shot him an irritated look. "Definitely!"

Joel turned again, and this time, his dark gaze flashed fire. She caught her breath, and he took half a step closer, eating up those last few inches between them. He didn't touch her, but the air between them seemed electric, and she could almost blame the storm outside for the way goose bumps ran up her arms. As if in response, a crack of lightning flashed outside the window.

Joel didn't flinch. "You make it sound like we had a choice in how we felt about each other. In our actions—yes. But falling in love with you? I was as helpless as a newborn kitten."

"Oh..." she whispered.

"I was a weak-willed man. I should have had the strength to wait for our baptisms and a wedding. I am ashamed of myself for encouraging you to break our promises we'd made to ourselves when it came to those relationship limits. But I loved you, and I've never felt anything even remotely similar since. I *loved* you."

Claire let out a slow breath. "Then how could you pal around with me as if I was nothing else to you?"

"It's not ideal," he said. "But it's better than nothing."

"I don't think I could handle it, Joel."

"That's fair enough," he said.

"And that isn't because I'm angry." Somehow, she wanted to clarify her feelings...even if only for herself.

"You might still be a little angry," he said. "And I can understand it."

"Maybe a tiny bit." She smiled, softening the words. "I'm working on that."

Joel nodded toward the staircase. "Let me finish the dishes. You go on up to bed."

Claire was about to argue with him—this was her kitchen, after all—but then he raised an eyebrow, and she felt her cheeks heat. There was still something about this man that made her melt just a little bit, and that was dangerous ground. She'd be wise to go up to bed and put some distance between them.

"All right, I will," she said softly.

"Good night." His dark gaze met hers once more, and Claire turned and headed for the stairs.

Yes, some distance between them was for the best—some distance and some time in prayer to get her balance back. Her anger that was draining away had served as her protection. An open, vulnerable heart was not a good idea with this man!

Joel Beiler had been her weakness five years ago, and she couldn't let him be her weakness again.

Joel listened to the sound of Claire's footsteps and then heard the creak of her door as it closed. He let out a slow breath. If only he could wall his heart off to her, but he'd never been able to.

She'd mentioned that letter from a farmer out in Oregon yesterday, and he knew that he of all people had no right to feel jealous. He wasn't offering her marriage, and she should find a husband of her own. But somehow, the idea of her marrying another man stabbed more deeply than it should.

Claire was beautiful, smart and there was something about her clear gaze that sent his heart tumbling. But he wasn't the same strong man he used to be. What would he do—offer her a future with a man who already couldn't do the men's work properly and who would very likely have another stroke? She needed a man, not a liability.

That massive stroke that had debilitated him so badly hadn't been the last one. There had been two more—significantly milder, but still. They were enough to give him a glimpse into the future. Some people could live long lives on the medication, and everything would be fine. Some—like him and his dad—had more complications. The doctors didn't know why he didn't respond as well to the medication, but they did say he'd probably have a similar experience to his father's.

Joel rinsed the last of the cutlery, then let the water out of the sink. He wrung out the cloth and hung it up the way his *mamm* at home insisted upon. He stood there in the soft light of the kerosene lamp, watching the trees out the window—what he could see of them—thrashing in the high wind.

"*Gott* give me strength..." he murmured.

It had been a bitter pill to lose his muscular physique, but physical strength wasn't what he needed most right now. He needed to keep his heart secure so that he could give Claire what she needed as a friend and be in his son's life somehow.

He turned off the kerosene lamp, and outside lightning flashed again, illuminating the kitchen for a split second that left spots in front of his eyes. A moment later, thunder boomed overhead.

It was a storm, all right, and he was grateful for it. Without this storm, he wouldn't have any chance to talk with Claire more deeply, or to play games with his bored son. Sometimes *Gott* worked in mysterious ways, using fish to swallow men or storms to lock them in. Sometimes *Gott* didn't calm the storm—he brought His child through it.

Joel went into his guest suite. Claire's touch

was evident around the place—some little woven baskets on a desktop that held useful items like face cloths, some individually wrapped hard-candy mints, and tiny bottles of hand cream, shampoo and conditioner to be used upstairs in the bathroom, presumably.

The bed had been remade—he'd made it this morning, but not quite so neatly as it looked now. There was no chocolate on his pillow this time, though, and he was mildly disappointed to see that. He shouldn't have mentioned it before.

Joel started a fire in the woodstove in his room, patiently stoking it to life until it crackled merrily, and he shut the stove door to let it burn. In a few minutes the whole room was pleasantly warm, and he got into his pajamas and put his clothes aside with his bag. Then he pulled out his little Bible and read a few passages before crawling into the cool, clean sheets.

He lay there in the darkness, listening to the howl of the wind and the patter of rain against his window. This storm would eventually blow out, and he'd have to make the best of the time he had here with Claire. If she was going to trust him to be in his son's life at all, he'd have to convince Claire.

He wouldn't hurt her. He wouldn't let her down, and he wouldn't disappoint Aaron, either. Would she be able to see his pure intentions?

Somehow, even with his whirling thoughts, Joel drifted off to sleep, and he dreamed of harvest season. He was on the wagon, slinging bales of hay into a neat pile to bring back to the barn, and as he worked, he realized that he was strong again—young, tough, muscled. For a moment, he was in awe of his newfound abilities, but then being whole became normal, nothing unexpected, and he continued to work, laughing along with some jokes his brother was telling…

That dream melted away, and in its place was another dream of water falling, dripping, pooling… In his dream, he was doing dishes out there in Claire's kitchen, and he couldn't get the tap to turn off. The water kept pouring out, overflowing the sink and puddling on the floor, and he was filled with panic. He woke up in a sweat, and it took him a moment to realize that the sound of water he heard was from outside, not indoors. It was water draining out of the eaves into an overflowing rain barrel outside his window. He lay there in the dark, his heart still thudding hard as his body caught up with reality.

Lightning flashed, brightening the room in a flicker of light, then going dark again. A second later there was a boom of thunder. Then more lightning, followed half a heartbeat later by thunder again.

That lightning was close, and the thunder rattled the windows. Then another crack of lightning, a heart-stopping boom, and Joel looked out the window as orange sparks shot out into the darkness and a deafening crack filled the air. A tree had been hit—he knew the sound—and then there was the sound of scraping tree branches against the house and a thud overhead. Joel went to the window, leaning as far to the side as he could, but he couldn't make out much more than the soft glow of burned wood where lightning had struck a tree next to the house. That was close! He sent up an instinctive prayer, thanking *Gott* for His mercies.

Joel heard feet hitting the floor overhead, and he headed for the door to his room. As he plunged out into the dark kitchen, Ted and Gloria came down the stairs, Gloria in a long flannel nightgown and Ted wearing a pair of jeans and a blanket thrown over his shoulders.

"What was that?" Gloria's hair was flattened and mussed, and without her makeup, she looked softer somehow.

"Did lightning hit the house?" Ted tugged his blanket closer around his shoulders.

"I think it hit the tree beside the house," Joel said. "I could see the burn mark on it."

"Something definitely hit the house," Ted countered. "I heard something on the roof."

Claire came down then, Aaron clinging to her long flannel nightgown next to her. The dog followed behind them. She had a lit kerosene lantern in one hand and walked purposefully up to the hook above the table and suspended it there. Aaron sat down on the stairs and leaned tiredly against the large dog.

"I think we have a tree limb on the roof," Claire said. "It landed just above my bed."

"Is there any damage you can see?" Joel asked. "Cracks in the wall plaster, anything like that?"

"Not that I noticed, but I'll look closer in the light of day," Claire replied, and then she rallied herself. "Everyone, it's going to be fine. The storm is still blowing out there, but as long as we have walls and a roof, we'll be fine until it stops. This is a problem for later."

"You should get that branch off the roof, though," Ted said. "They can do a lot of damage to shingles, at the very least."

"Well, we can't do it tonight." Claire suppressed a yawn.

"I'll take care of it tomorrow," Joel said.

"You will?" Claire clamped her mouth shut as if biting back further words.

Right. The words had come out of his mouth before he could stop them. He was thinking like he was still a big, strong man who could go up there and wrestle that limb off the roof for her barehanded.

Joel lowered his voice. "I might be able to do something, at least." The Wassels moved over to the staircase again.

"We'll head back up to bed, then," Ted said.

"Yes." Claire cast them a smile. "I'm sorry for the disturbance. It will be fine. Good night. Sleep well."

The *Englisher* couple went back up the stairs. Joel eyed Claire. She looked calm, unruffled…except for a slight tremble in her hands. She was shaken but trying to hide it.

"Hey…" He crossed the room and caught her trembling fingers in his. "Are you okay?"

Claire sighed. "I told Adel I could take care of this place like Naomi did. And you'd have to know Naomi to understand why that was very forward of me. Naomi had contacts, connections, people who loved to help her. And she was strong, smart and could fix pretty much anything."

"I'm sure you're competent, too," he said. "Would Naomi fix the roof?"

"No, but she'd know who to ask for a quote," she said. "I'm competent, but if I have to keep calling Adel's husband up here to take care of things, I'm not going to be quite as competent as I need to be. This job—managing this place—is my ticket, Joel. If I can run this bed-and-breakfast efficiently and help it to grow, then I can have a safe and cozy home to raise my son, and I won't be pushed into any corners with marriages."

"This storm isn't your fault." Joel met her gaze.

"I know, and Adel is fair, of course, but I don't want her having to send someone else in to help me run this place. I really want to do it on my own."

Joel nodded. "Okay. I get it. I meant it when I said I'd take care of whatever is up on the roof."

"Joel..." she said softly.

She wasn't going to believe any of his bravado, and maybe that was for the best. It was time to be realistic here.

"I can't do it by myself anymore," he conceded. "I'll definitely need a hand with it, but if you'll help me, I figure together, between the two of us, we can take care of it."

Claire brightened. "Okay. *Yah.* Let's go up there in the morning, as long as the lightning is past, and clear it up. You're sure you'll be okay?"

"I'm sure," he said. *Gott* willing, at least, he'd be able to be like Samson and rally his strength for just one more job. For Claire.

"Okay. Thank you, Joel."

"No problem."

Claire held a hand out to Aaron. "Come on, Aaron. Up to bed. It's the middle of the night, son."

"Can I come to your bed?" Aaron looked up at her, eyes wide and scared.

"Sure. Just for tonight."

Claire reached up and turned off the kerosene lamp, leaving them in the low light of the storm outside.

"Good night, Joel."

"Good night."

He watched her go back up the stairs, their son's hand in hers. If he'd sent word to her when he was in the hospital, this might be his home with Claire, or one similar, and he might be raising his son with her.

But then he'd be one more worry for her to handle, one more burden on her shoulders. In his mind's eye, he saw his mother slipping on her shoes and marching out that door. It made his chest clench even now to remember it.

A man counted on the woman in his family to stand by him, to take care of his needs and comforts, to love him when he felt unlovable. If his own mother could march out that door, completely burned-out by all the pressures of her family, then it was only a matter of time before Claire would do the same. The pressures would be pretty similar.

No, he wouldn't be that burden on her shoulders. He'd make things easier where he could. It was the least he could offer her.

Chapter Six

Claire could hear the tree branch scraping on the roof whenever the wind howled loudest, and she sent up a prayer that Gott would protect their roof. Aaron snuggled up next to her, and she wrapped her arm around her son, feeling the tickle of his rumpled hair against her face. Goliath, or Ollie, as his Englisher owners called him, lay on the floor next to the bed.

Aaron was growing up. He was nearly five, and while she wouldn't send him to the first grade for another year, this last year of keeping him at home felt precious. Every day he seemed either a little taller or just a little older. He learned new words or expressed himself in an older way. She and Naomi used to joke that Aaron would never grow up, and they would never grow old, but that wasn't going to happen. Aaron was sprouting in front of her very eyes.

If it weren't for this storm, Claire would have gone to talk to someone about this situation—gotten some wisdom from a friend. Adel would be an ideal source of advice. Her friend Sarai would be a sympathetic ear, even if she didn't have the life experience to dip into that Adel had. And Claire needed some strength from her friends right now, because the thought of Joel leaving, as he would have to do shortly, was starting to tear at her heart in a way that scared her. She was getting attached…again! Feeling more for Joel was a very bad idea, and yet she'd always been drawn to him, even now when he'd lost that muscular physique. She still felt more for him than she should. Was it just that he was the father of her precious boy, or was it something more?

This was why she needed her friends! She needed them to help her sort it all out.

Whatever these feelings were, she needed to get them under control, because Joel had stayed away for the last five years for a reason.

Claire smoothed her son's hair down from where it was tickling her nose, and her gaze moved toward the dresser, where that letter from Adam Lantz waited. The farmer from Oregon needed his answer, too, and Claire lay silently in the dark, thinking about that letter with the straightforward questions from a man in want of a wife.

That was a man who was looking to commit!

Gott, if Joel hadn't come, this would be easier, she prayed silently. *What do I do? Is Adam Lantz for me? I wish You'd tell me! Make it clear, take away the guessing...*

But Gott didn't give her a clear answer. It was just a letter, loaded with possibility and sitting in her top drawer next to her *kapps* and her good Sunday apron.

Aaron squirmed around to get a more comfortable position, which ended up with his bony posterior in her stomach, and she blinked into the darkness. Overhead, the wind moaned, and the limb on the roof ground against the shingles in an unsettling way. She exhaled a slow breath. There was nothing that could be done until morning.

Gott, guide me, she prayed in her heart, and she finally fell back asleep to the sound of the rain lashing the windows and Aaron's even breathing.

When the sky lightened to a rainy dawn,

Claire got up, easing her arm out from underneath her sleeping son and sliding his knee away from her ribs. Her arm tingled from not moving for so long, and she grabbed her dress and *kapp* and sneaked out to the bathroom to get dressed and washed up before starting her day.

The rain had lessened now and was coming down in a soft drizzle, and when she got down to the kitchen, neatly dressed, she looked out the side window at the muddy ground and deep pools of water covering the drive. The Wassels' car's tires were submerged all the way up to the undercarriage, and Claire winced. She didn't know much about cars, but she couldn't imagine that would be good for it.

She started the fires in both the cooking stove and the potbellied stove used to heat the house. Once they were both burning nicely, the door to the guest suite opened, and Joel came into the kitchen. He was fully dressed and looked like he'd shaved as well, using the washbasin she'd left for him in his room.

"Good morning," she said.

"Good morning. How'd you sleep after that rude awakening last night?"

"Not as well as I could have," she said with a rueful smile.

"Was Aaron afraid of the storm?" he asked.

"Not when he was in bed with me," she replied. "He spread out, stuck a knee in my side and slept like a baby."

Joel laughed. "He's sleeping still?"

She nodded and pulled down a pot for oatmeal. "I'll get some oatmeal on the stove, and we can eat before we go up to the roof. As long as it doesn't start pouring again."

The sooner that fallen limb was off the roof, the better she'd feel.

Breakfast didn't take long, and by the time Claire and Joel had finished eating, Aaron and the Wassels had come downstairs. Claire dashed back up with Gloria to help her get dressed in one of Claire's cape dresses.

Claire bent down in front of Gloria, pushing the straight pins into the waistline of the dress to keep it snug.

"There." Claire inserted the last pin and stood back to inspect her handiwork. "That should do it."

"It's quite comfortable," Gloria said. "My hair is a mess, though. What I wouldn't give for a flat iron right about now."

Claire chuckled. "Your hair isn't long enough for a bun, but maybe a little ponytail?"

Soon enough, Gloria was neatly arranged

in as much Amish clothing as was appropriate. Her cheeks pinked when she looked at herself in the full-length mirror.

"I look older without my makeup," Gloria said.

"I think you look lovely," Claire said. "More natural."

"You're sweet, Claire," Gloria said. "For us regular folks, getting older is something we fight. Youthfulness at all costs. I'm not saying it's healthy, or that we women even like the pressure, but it's there. I think it's good to just see the way the good Lord made you and accept it. I'm sure you Amish women are happier for it."

"For us, we're grateful for the years *Gott* gives us," Claire said. "And for our children and husbands…"

Claire felt a tightening in her throat at the last word, and she sighed. Yes, she would be grateful if one day *Gott* provided her a husband of her own, but it would take a leap of bravery for her to accomplish it. Had she been rash in asking Adel to help her find a match? Should she have waited on *Gott* to bring it about in His time?

"We're grateful for those things, too, of course." Gloria followed Claire out of the bedroom. "It has to do with what people compliment you on, you know? 'You look so great for your age,' or 'your skin is so smooth' or 'you look ten years younger than you are'… and it's makeup. It's not real! What do you compliment each other about?"

Claire paused at the top of the stairway.

"Our cooking, being able to make a difficult dish, our needlework, our children…" Claire sighed. "Basically, it's the role of a wife—and if you aren't a wife… Well, I suppose I understand how compliments can leave you feeling less secure."

"It's the universal plight of women." Gloria leaned over and gave Claire a nudge. "We aren't so different, are we?"

Claire smiled at Gloria and led the way back downstairs. As she and Gloria walked into the kitchen, Joel and Ted looked up from where they sat at the table. Gloria's laugh filled the room.

"Ted, look at me!" She laughed. "How do you like it?"

"You, my dear, look about as fresh as a daisy."

"I do not," she said, but she smiled all the same. "I look like a grandmother."

"You are a grandmother." He winked. "A perfectly beautiful grandmother."

Aaron had set his wooden farm up on the sitting room floor again, food forgotten for the moment. Normally, Claire would insist upon eating at the proper time, but she didn't want to risk the skies opening up again and losing their window of opportunity.

"Should we get up to the roof while we can?" Joel asked.

"*Yah*, I think so," she agreed.

"Where do you keep the ladder?" Joel asked.

"In the basement," Claire said. "I'll show you."

They went down the steps together, Joel's limp more evident this morning than it had been before. He seemed to balance against the handrail as he made his way down with her into the unfinished basement. She almost asked him if this chore would be too much for him, but she stopped herself. Joel's physical abilities might have altered, but his male pride had not.

"There." She pointed to where the ladder leaned against the wall next to the wringer washer. Joel picked up one end, and Claire hurried forward to grab the other end.

"Claire, let me carry it."

"It's heavy, though," she countered. Joel didn't have the strength he used to, but he still had that direct stare of his that used to turn her stomach to butterflies, and she smiled faintly.

"I'm not the pretty girl you used to flirt with anymore, Joel." He didn't need to impress her.

"Sure you are." Joel winked, then hoisted the ladder up under his good arm. "I'm still a man, Claire. You have to let me act like one."

"All right, then." She put her hands up.

Joel started up the stairs, and she could see the effort it took for him to carry the heavy ladder. His gallantry might make today easier, but it would make their eventual parting harder.

"I didn't have breakfast, *Mamm*," Aaron said as they emerged from the basement.

Claire felt her heart sink, and she looked toward the hot stove. Aaron was too young to navigate a woodstove alone safely, and that lull in the rain would only last so long.

"Are you hungry?" Gloria stood up. "I can get him breakfast, Claire. It's no problem."

"Would you?" Claire asked. "I don't normally put my guests to work."

"I love kids," Gloria said. "I'm happy to

do it. Come on, Aaron. I'll get you some oatmeal, okay?"

Aaron happily followed Gloria to the stove.

"There's an apron in the top drawer by the sink," Claire called.

"Got it!" Gloria called back.

"Do you want a hand?" Ted asked.

"No, no, I've got it." Joel met the older man's gaze, and some unspoken communication seemed to pass between them, because Ted gave a nod and sank back into his chair.

Claire pulled on a raincoat, and Joel took his jacket down from the peg. They headed outside into the blustery wind, but the rain was nothing more than a mist against her face, and Claire let her hood fall back away from her head.

The tree that the lightning had struck was charred black on one side, and when she looked up at the roof, she discovered that it wasn't a limb that had fallen—it was half the tree! Claire stared up, her heart hammering in her chest.

"Let's get up there," Joel said grimly. "Do you have a saw? I need to cut off that last piece of wood that's still connected to the tree."

"Can we do it?" she asked, her earlier enthusiasm waning.

"*Yah*, we can do it. And the sooner the better. The wind might move it around on the roof and tear up the shingles."

They put the ladder up against the side of the house, and Claire then turned and waded across the muddy puddles to the stable and grabbed the saw from where it hung on a wall of tools. When she got back to the house, Joel was already on the roof.

Claire climbed up the ladder, the saw tucked under one arm, and when she got to the roof, Joel caught her hand to help her get up safely.

"I could hear that scraping last night." Claire looked at the fractured half of a tree. The wind whipped up suddenly, and Claire ducked her head and bent down to keep her footing. The tree swayed in the gale, and it scraped loudly against the shingles.

Joel wordlessly took the saw and headed over to the edge of the house. He knelt down on the roof—the movement to get him down looking awkward—and he started to saw with quick, strong strokes.

The wind whipped up again, and Claire went over to where he knelt, putting her weight against the limb to keep it stable while he worked. Sawing through the last of the splintered wood didn't take long. The next time the wind howled past them, there was no more risk of the branches tearing at the shingles.

Joel moved up the segment of tree and began sawing a branch. He stopped after a moment, resting, then started up again. When that limb came free, Claire picked it up and threw it clear of the roof onto the sodden grass below. Not too far in the distance, she saw the gray veil of approaching rain.

"That should do it." Joel pushed himself to his feet again. His weaker leg slipped underneath him, and Claire grabbed his arm to catch him.

"Sorry." Joel muttered, and he pulled free of her. "I'm fine."

"We're also on a roof, Joel," she said. "You shouldn't get too proud."

"Are you planning on carrying me down?" He shot her a rueful smile. "Maybe over your shoulder like a calf?"

Claire chuckled. "No. That wasn't the plan."

"Then you'd better let me stand on my own two feet, Claire." Joel reached out and touched her cheek tenderly.

The movement was a familiar one, and she

froze, his warm fingers lingering on her jaw in a way she remembered. Joel seemed to realize what he'd done, because his face colored, and he smiled faintly and dropped his hand.

"I'm not your girlfriend anymore, Joel," she said quietly.

"I know."

"It will look bad to people." It was the quickest excuse she could think of.

"To whom?" He looked around them. She knew what he was seeing—the expanse of farmland separating them from the neighbors on either side. She felt her throat tighten.

"It will make it harder for me when you leave, Joel. Don't do that. I used to love you."

And she was trying very hard not to love him again. She wasn't his to touch, to hold, to smile at like that. She wasn't his to treat like he loved her when he didn't. Her heart couldn't navigate those games.

"I'm sorry," he said softly. "I won't do that again." He paused for a moment. "I know you don't want to take any chances here, but we can stay in touch, at least. Maybe we could write to each other."

His voice was low and gentle…far too tempting.

"Joel, you can't play games with me like that."

"I'm not playing."

"Then maybe I just take things more seriously than you ever do." She pushed a loose tendril of hair off her cheek. "But I can't be the woman waiting on your letters."

Because if he said he'd write, she'd wait, she'd check the mail, she'd endure disappointment every time it was empty… No, her heart couldn't go halfway. And after him leaving her the first time, that hope would just be pathetic. The rumble of thunder sounded closer than before, a few drops of rain splattering around them.

"Okay… I won't write, then." There was a catch in his voice that betrayed deeper feeling.

"It isn't fair!"

"I won't do anything that would make your life harder." He looked at her tenderly. "That's a promise."

"Okay." And she wasn't sure if she was glad or disappointed to hear he wouldn't write. Her heart seemed determined to feel pain regardless of what this man did.

Joel bent down and hoisted up one end of the limb. Claire took the other end of the broken tree, and they carried it to the edge of the roof. The smudge of approaching rain was a whole lot closer now, looking like a gray veil descending from boiling black clouds.

"Carefully now." Joel gazed warily in the direction of that oncoming storm. "On the count of three..."

They heaved it over the side. It fell beside the house, where the water had gathered with a splash, and thunder rumbled again.

Joel angled his head toward the ladder. "Let's get this off the roof."

Claire let him go ahead of her, and Joel backed down the ladder. When he reached the bottom, he held it for her. She tucked her dress around her knees and started down, but the wind was blowing harder now, and icy bullets of fresh rain splattered against her face. When she got halfway down, she felt the ladder slip, heard Joel's gasp, and she suddenly dropped.

Joel's arm came around her waist as she plummeted toward the ground, and they fell together in a heap in the middle of a muddy puddle. She lay still for a moment, wondering if she was hurt, but Joel had broken her fall. She could feel him breathing underneath her. She quickly rolled off him.

"I'm okay." She pushed herself to her knees in the middle of the chilly water and then to her feet. Water trickled down her legs and into her boots. "I'm muddy but okay."

She looked down at Joel then, and Claire's heart thudded to a stop. Pain twisted his features. His bad knee was folded underneath him, and he grimaced as he pushed himself off his leg.

"Joel!"

He touched his knee gingerly. "My knee—"

Joel might have broken her fall, but he was hurt, and she crouched down next to him, afraid to touch him but wanting to help somehow.

"I thought I had you," Joel said through gritted teeth. "I really thought I had you."

Pain made Joel's stomach roll, but he could feel Claire tugging at his arm. He let out a pent-up breath and looked up to see Ted hurrying out of the house toward them, his head ducked against the rain. Ted hooked a hand under Joel's arm, and Claire took the other, and they helped him to his feet.

He'd been so certain when he leaped forward that his body would do what his instincts told him to do—catch her! Five years ago, he could have caught her without a problem, and now…she'd slid through his arms, and he'd felt the crumbling reality of his limitations.

It was humiliating.

Rain had started to fall in earnest, and Joel limped painfully between Claire and Ted up the steps and into the house. Claire peeled off her coat—her dress was dripping with muddy water, but she didn't seem to notice. She and Ted helped Joel over to a kitchen chair, and he sank into it gratefully.

When Joel closed his eyes, he was still the big quarter horse of a man—that was the bitter irony. His current physical state was new enough that his mind hadn't caught up with it yet. But when he opened his eyes, he was this much frailer version of himself…not muscled enough to do more than break Claire's fall. He wanted to be her hero, not a cushion in the mud. The blow to his pride hurt worse than his twisted knee, and that was saying something.

"*Mamm! Mamm!* Are you hurt?" Aaron tugged at his mother's arm. "*Mamm!*"

Joel undid his coat, and Claire tugged it off his shoulders, letting it drop to the bottom of the chair. Heat from the potbellied woodstove pumped toward him in a comforting wave, and he let out a slow breath.

"I'm fine, sweetie." Claire turned toward the boy. "I'm just fine."

"I saw a tree branch fall, and then another one, and then I saw *you* fall, *Mamm*!"

Aaron must have been watching from the window. Joel couldn't blame him—it was the most interesting thing happening that morning.

"Are you okay?" Aaron peered up into Joel's face questioningly.

"I'm okay." Joel winced as he tried to adjust his position on the chair.

"Stop moving," Claire ordered. "Aaron, I want you to run upstairs and get me the old sheet I use for scraps. It's it the linen closet. You know the one."

Aaron clattered up the stairs, and Claire bent down in front of Joel and pushed his pant leg up above his knee. She felt his knee gingerly with her cool fingers. Ted and Gloria stood back, watching with stricken expressions on their faces. How bad did he look, exactly, to cause that kind of reaction?

"It's a twisted knee," Joel said. "I won't die."

Gloria smiled faintly. "It just looks painful. Can I get you something, Joel?"

"I'm okay."

"A cookie?" Gloria pressed, and tears suddenly welled in her eyes. "Joel, I'm a mother whose son would have been your age, okay? I need to get you something."

Joel blinked up at her. Right. She'd lost a son, and here he was looking about as strong and manly as a newborn calf.

"Uh—" He forced a smile. "A cookie would be great, Gloria."

Ted cast Joel a grateful look, and he followed his wife into the kitchen.

"Did you figure out the oatmeal?" Claire called after them.

"Yes, just waiting for it to boil," Gloria replied.

"Do you think you could fill the kettle for tea? I'm sure you can figure it out with the woodstove, can't you?" she asked. In control, thinking ahead—it was clear that this was Claire's domain.

Claire sat back on her haunches and regarded Joel mutely. Gone were the days when she looked up at him with hope in her eyes, believing he could do just about anything. She used to make him feel like a giant of a man. There was sympathy in her gaze now.

"I used to be able to catch you," Joel said quietly.

She'd slipped from the back of a wagon once, and he'd scooped her up before her feet even touched the ground. She'd been light as a feather, and he'd been…he'd been capable. He'd known beyond a doubt that he could protect her, provide for her, make her happy.

"Oh, Joel. We were both younger then."

"It was only five years, and in my head, like on an instinctive level… I'm still that man. When I went to catch you, I honestly thought… I would."

"I'm just glad nothing is broken." She smiled wanly. "I'm not as small as I used to be, either, Joel. I'm a *mamm* now."

"You're still pretty small." He returned her smile with a pained one of his own. "You aren't the one who changed. Let's not pretend that, okay?"

Aaron came back down the stairs with a folded sheet, and she rose to her feet then and ripped a long strip from the cloth and crouched down in front of Joel once more.

"Your cookie." Gloria passed him a chocolate chip cookie with tears in her eyes.

"Thank you, Gloria." He tried to look grateful for the cookie, because he could tell it meant a lot to her.

She headed back into the kitchen, where

her husband was filling a kettle, leaving them alone again.

"She sees her son when she looks at me," Joel said, his voice low.

Claire nodded. "I think so. You're hurt...he died in an accident. And the timing—" Claire looked toward the couple in the kitchen, then turned her attention back to Joel's leg. "Straighten your leg." She started to wrap his knee, her fingers pressing lightly against his skin as she worked. "When I see little boys get hurt playing baseball or falling, my heart does that same thing for them that it does for Aaron. It's the way *Gott* made mothers."

"Is that what you're doing to me right now?" he asked. "Mothering me?"

Pink touched her cheeks. "No."

"You sure?" He meant to tease, but somehow the moment deepened in spite of his attempts to lighten it. She paused, her blue eyes moving up to meet his, and his breath caught in his chest.

"I was never your mother."

No, she'd never been that. He swallowed, and she turned her attention back to wrapping the bandage, and he noticed that their son had sidled up closer to watch the work. He'd better be more careful what he said.

"You got hurt." Aaron leaned against Joel's chair. "Again."

"*Yah.*" Joel hated this. Claire was the one who'd fallen, and he was the one getting the sympathy. "Except the first time I fell, and this time, your mother fell on top of me."

He shot Aaron a grin.

"Maybe I can get you some ice—that will help." Claire rolled her eyes at him as she tucked the end of the cloth under the wrapped bandage.

"I don't need the ice." He bent his knee and tested the pain. The tension really did help, and he didn't want to be mollycoddled any more than he had to be. Gloria was already standing sentry over the teapot, and he had a feeling if he let this go much further, he'd end up with a pillow and a lap blanket like an old man.

"Yes, you do need ice." Claire's tone firmed. "Ice makes a big difference."

"Do you want a spoonful of sugar to go with your cookie?" Aaron asked hopefully.

"No, I don't need sugar, either." He shot his son a rueful smile. "Sugar is for little kids."

"I don't see why!" Aaron argued. "Sugar can be for grown-ups, too!"

Joel looked over his shoulder toward the

door. The animals still needed to be cared for this morning, and he felt a surge of frustration. Aaron went over to the counter and came back with a bowl of sugar and a teaspoon. He held a heaping spoonful in front of Joel.

"Open," Aaron commanded.

"Wha—?" Joel started to say, and Aaron slipped the spoon between his lips with a satisfied smile. Joel caught the dusting of sugar that spilled down his chin in one cupped hand and pulled the spoon out of his mouth. The sugar melted on his tongue.

"It helps, right?" Aaron beamed.

Was this the sign he should just give up and accept his lot as old man around here?

"Kind of," Joel admitted grudgingly, swallowing. "But a man doesn't take sugar when he's hurt. He just deals with it."

"Does he take ice?" Claire held up a plastic bag filled with ice cubes, a small smile turning up one side of her lips.

Joel knew when he was beaten. If he had any dignity left, it had dissolved with that teaspoon of sugar.

"Fine, I'll take the ice." He held his hand out for the bag. Aaron's eyes suddenly locked on Joel's arm, and he shot a hand out to stop Joel's movement.

"You have a strawberry on your arm, too!" Aaron exclaimed. "I have one, see?"

The boy pulled up his sleeve and held out his arm. Right in the same place that Joel had a pink birthmark, Aaron had one, too. It was the same shape, the same color, the same place... Joel's heart hammered to a stop in his chest, and he looked up at Claire.

She'd gone white, and she planted a firm hand on Aaron's shoulder.

"Son, that's not polite to go showing off birthmarks." Her voice sounded much more in control than her face looked. "I want you to take that scrap sheet upstairs and fold it for me, okay?"

"By myself?"

"Do the best you can," she replied. "Off you go." And when Aaron paused, she added more firmly, "Now, Aaron."

The boy trudged off toward the stairs, the sheet in a bundle under one arm. Joel dragged his gaze back to Claire. That hadn't been his fault—Aaron had spotted the birthmark on his own. Claire's lips had gone white, and she put a hand on his arm, as if to hold herself up.

"I'm sorry," Joel murmured.

"He won't understand," she said softly.

Joel put the ice onto his knee, and the cold did feel good against the aching joint. Claire was right—Aaron wouldn't understand what a shared birthmark meant. Not yet. But she made that sound like a good thing.

Had it occurred to Claire that he might have a heart, too? She was protecting their son, but Joel's heart had wrapped around both Claire and Aaron already.

Gloria came up to the table with a cup rattling on a saucer and a teary smile on her face.

"There." Gloria slid the cup next to him on the tabletop. "Tea. Drink up. It helps."

It was a maternal gift of comfort that this *Englisher* woman hadn't been able to give to her own son. Joel did the only thing he could—he lifted the cup to his lips and took a sip.

Chapter Seven

Later that evening, Joel sat by the window and watched the lantern light flickering through the gap in the open stable door outside through the rain. Claire was out there doing the chores, and Aaron had gone along "to help Mamm." Gloria stood at the sink washing dishes, looking so much like an Amish woman in that pink cape dress. Gloria seemed to be the dog's second-favorite person around here, because he lay on the floor by her feet.

And Joel sat here by the window, watching that flicker of light from the stable and wishing his knee would bear weight right now so he could get out there and do the men's chores. But he couldn't, and he hated it.

A long time ago, his own father had sat by

windows, glaring outside balefully, watching his mother weed the garden, and Joel could understand it now. His father used to be a big man, too, and after the strokes, he'd deteriorated before their eyes. Had he ever gotten used to his frailer state, or had he been like Joel, with the heart of a muscular man and a body that defied him? Was that where his father's constant simmering anger had come from—knowing what it felt like to be whole?

Joel pushed himself slowly to his feet and tested his knee. It was sore, and then there was his bad leg that didn't react like it should at the best of times. He put his weight on it and was able to hobble a couple of steps before he had to stop.

"Do you need something?" Ted asked. "I can grab it for you."

"No, I'm just trying to get moving," Joel said.

He'd been hoping that his leg would suddenly be better and he'd be able to head out to the stable to take over. That's what he'd been hoping.

"Yeah, I get it," Ted said. "You get to be my age, an injury like that could make you hobble around for months."

"I already do limp around," Joel said. "So this is just more frustration."

"What happened?" Ted sat at the table, and Joel joined him.

"I have a blood-clotting disorder that causes strokes and other medical issues. I've had a couple of strokes that I never fully recovered from. The first one was the worst."

"I'm sorry," Ted said. "That's terrible."

"That's life." Joel leaned back in the chair.

"Aaron—Claire's boy," Ted said. "He's your son, isn't he?"

Joel looked over at the man in shock. "What?"

"I can tell it's a big secret." Ted shrugged. "But he looks like you, and I noticed those matching birthmarks before Aaron did. There's only one thing that explains it."

So much for keeping this under wraps. Joel looked down at his arm and rubbed a hand over the pink mark. A strawberry, his son had called it. That would have been from Claire. She used to call his birthmark the same thing.

"Yeah, he's mine." Joel pulled his sleeve back down. "I only found out when I arrived. I didn't know about him. If I had, trust me, I wouldn't have just left them on their own."

Ted nodded. "I'm not judging."

"Maybe I am." Joel sighed. "He looks like me?"

"A lot, yeah."

"My *mamm* said I had blond hair when I was little, so that might be from my side of the family."

"My son looked like me, too," Ted said quietly. "He was a spitting image. If you looked at pictures of Royden and I at the same age—say, high school—the only way you could tell us apart was by the clothing."

"That's amazing," Joel said.

"Yeah." Ted cleared his throat. "A son—the Bible talks about how a man is blessed if he has sons, and I love my daughter just as much as I loved Royden, but a son is a special relationship. A son learns how to be a man from his father."

An opportunity Joel was missing out on with Aaron. Would another man show Aaron what it meant to be good, honest and reliable? Would Aaron grow up in Oregon with a different community and a stepfather? The thought made Joel's chest tighten. Was this jealousy or protectiveness?

"What happened between you and Claire?" Ted asked.

"I didn't know I'd fathered Aaron." Joel sighed. "I meant to come back for her, but I had that first bad stroke, and it took me months to relearn how to talk, let alone feed myself. I couldn't go back like that."

"She waited?"

Joel nodded. "It seems."

"She loved you."

"Back then she did, yes," Joel said. "Now? Let's just say I wasn't a pleasant surprise."

Ted nodded slowly. "I broke Gloria's heart once."

"Oh?" Joel looked over at the man in surprise.

"I called off the wedding," Ted said. "Obviously, it was stupid. I was listening to my cousins, who were warning me about getting married and having a woman run my life. I was young—so was Gloria. They told me not to get married yet. So I very stupidly told Gloria I wasn't ready for marriage and called off the wedding."

"Oh." Joel winced. "How far before?"

"A month," Ted said. "I came to my senses the next day, and when I went back to Gloria, she wasn't so easily won back. I'd hurt her. And she'd already told her parents and sisters that I'd called it off."

"So what did you do?"

"I did what any good man would do in that situation." Ted grinned. "I begged."

Ted chuckled at his own humor, but Joel couldn't see the funny part in this tale.

"And she took you back?"

"Yep. Thankfully." Ted glanced into the kitchen toward his wife. "And I was never so foolish again. I learned then that you should never take relationship advice from single guys. They have no idea what they're talking about."

"Sound advice." Joel smiled.

"Remember it. You'll save yourself a lot of grief, I assure you." Ted was silent for a moment. "So, are you here to marry Claire?"

Joel let out a slow breath. "No. And I know how bad that sounds, but Claire can do better than me. She's got a matchmaker here who has someone lined up. I'm not the man she fell in love with anymore." Ted was silent, and Joel looked up at him. "You are judging me now."

"No," Ted replied. "I was just thinking how universal all of this is—love, children, marriage. You and I come from completely different cultures, but the important stuff is the same."

They sat in silence for a couple of minutes, just two men sitting side by side, watching tea steam in front of them.

"I didn't know my dad growing up," Ted said after a few beats of silence.

"Why not?"

"He left when I was little." Ted spread his hands. "My mother told me that they argued a lot, and he eventually just left. So I grew up with a stepdad."

"A good stepfather?"

"Good. Yes." Ted sighed. "But he never did feel like my real father. I knew my dad left us. And he never came back. Never wanted to see me grow up…never contributed to my education. Nothing. That was tough for me growing up, especially when my mom would say I sounded just like him or I looked like him."

"You were angry?" Joel curled his fingers around the hot mug.

"I was confused." Ted sucked in a breath. "My father contacted me when I was in my thirties, married with kids of my own. He was dying of lung cancer and wanted to connect before he passed."

"And?"

"And…it was like looking in the mirror," Ted said, "if I'd made poorer choices. But I got to make my peace with him before he died."

"For what it's worth, I'm going to be giving Claire money to help her out," Joel said. A lot of money, actually. "And if she'll let me, I want to be in my son's life."

"I don't mean to guilt you," Ted said, "but realize that a kid grows up and comes to his own conclusions. We might want them to see it from our perspective, but they never do."

"I don't know what else to do," Joel admitted.

"I don't have the answers for you, either," Ted said. "But just know what's in the balance here. That relationship between a father and his son is an important one. That's all I'm trying to say."

An important relationship, indeed. What was worse: An absent father who sent money or a present one who made a boy's mother miserable? What left a deeper scar?

Or were the scars just different?

Outside the window, Joel saw the bobbing light of a lantern coming back toward the house. He pushed himself to his feet and hobbled toward the side door. It opened before he could reach it, and Aaron came into the house first, followed by Claire with the lantern. She turned the knob, the light blinking out, and she put it up on a shelf and swung the door shut with a nudge from her hip.

"The horses are clean and happy," Claire said.

"And I gave your horse some oats." Aaron smiled.

"Thank you," Joel took a limping step back. "I appreciate that."

"How's the knee?" Claire asked.

"Improving," Joel said.

Aaron pulled off his boots and hung up his coat. "I'm doing men's chores. Because I'm much bigger now."

"Go wash up now." Claire chuckled. "Use the bathroom upstairs."

"Goliath!" Aaron called in Pennsylvania Dutch as he went into the kitchen. "Come on, Goliath!"

"The dog only understands English." Claire shook her head, but when Joel looked back, he saw the dog padding obediently after the boy, following him to the stairs.

"I don't know," Joel said. "He might be learning."

Claire leaned against the door frame, her coat still on, watching her son. Then she sighed.

"He's going to miss that dog."

"Do you think the owners might be willing to part with him?" Joel asked.

She fumbled in her coat pocket and pulled out a piece of paper folded into quarters. She handed it over to him, and he opened it. There was a picture of Goliath, or a dog that looked pretty similar, with his tongue lolling out and a happy lift to his tail.

Reward for the return of our beloved pet. Answers to Ollie. German shepherd with a fully black tail. Please help him come home. We miss him.

Beneath that was a phone number. That was a family longing to be reunited with a much-loved pet.

"They won't give him up," Joel said.

"No, they won't." Claire pressed her lips together. "It's good for Aaron to learn to do the right thing, but I hate seeing his heart broken."

"The right thing often hurts," he said softly.

The right thing often tore a heart right out. But what was the right thing for him right now? What was the choice that would be in his son's ultimate best interest, regardless of what it did to Joel?

Joel took a step, and his knee buckled. He grimaced—more from frustration than pain—and he caught himself on the door frame. His hand was planted above Claire's shoulder, and he found himself looking into those blue eyes, his lips a breath away from hers.

She was beautiful—maybe even more so than five years ago. He swallowed, and she dropped her gaze.

Five years ago, he would have kissed her.

Five years ago, she would have kissed him!

Things were different now. He pushed himself away from the door frame and took a hobbling step back. This wasn't about what he wanted anymore. It had to be about his son.

It had to be.

Claire felt Gloria and Ted's eyes on her as she eased away from Joel and headed back into the kitchen, her cheeks hot. Somehow, having him leaning over her like that, his dark gaze blazing down into hers, it was like those last five years had melted away out from under her, and the power of her old feelings for him had come back in a rush.

That had always been the problem with Joel. Falling into his arms had been too easy.

She walked briskly into the kitchen and stopped at the sink, wishing there was a load of dishes to wash or something to do. It was inconveniently clean! She turned on the water to wash her hands.

"Will someone play chutes and ladders with me?" Aaron asked hopefully.

"I'll play with you," Ted said. "And then maybe Joel will, too."

"Sure, I'll play second," Joel said.

She looked over her shoulder, and Joel's gaze flickered in her direction. He cast her a wry smile and then limped in the direction of the sitting room.

"I have my toy farm, too!" Aaron was saying as he led the way, his voice growing softer and more muffled as he disappeared into the other room.

Claire exhaled a soft sigh.

"If I'm not mistaken, that young man has feelings for you," Gloria said.

Claire dried her hands and turned to face the older woman.

"I know Joel Beiler rather well. He's not serious."

"But he thinks the world of you—you can

see it in his eyes when he looks at you," Gloria said.

"Do you think so?" Claire looked in the direction of the sitting room. "Sometimes men make their feelings appear more than they really are."

"He looks sincere to me," Gloria said. "But you're right. They can."

"You and your husband seem to have a strong marriage," Claire said. "Do you mind if I ask your secret?"

"Well, part of the secret is to marry the right man." Gloria smiled. "And only God can lead you there."

"That's the hard part," Claire replied. "What's the rest of the secret?"

"The other part is that you have to keep caring for your marriage, over all those bumps that life will cast your way. You never take it for granted. You treat it with the care and attention you'd give a rare treasure, because it really is just that. Ted is such a good man. Even when Royden died, he kept turning toward me, and we kept holding on to each other. We still had our daughter, Ashley, who needed us, and I think that helped, too. I know another couple who got divorced when their daughter died. They just couldn't find their stability again after that. So I don't take my husband for granted. Ever."

"Is that part of why you came basket weaving?" Claire asked.

Gloria nodded. "Yes. I've been going out of my way to find things Ted and I can do together...especially with this painful anniversary. Maybe I go overboard with it. I signed us up for ballroom dancing lessons last year, and we took some swimming lessons together...now it's basket weaving. I don't think Ted cares about any of these activities, honestly. He's happiest at home with the TV, but I lost my son, and there is no pain in my life that's ever come close. If I lost my husband, too, I don't know what I'd do. I want to do anything I can to keep our marriage strong, and maybe I try too hard."

But Claire hadn't even had the chance to try with Joel. Joel had left and decided that she couldn't handle those hard times before they even got that far. He'd loved her, but since when was that enough?

"I think trying at all is a wonderful thing," Claire said.

If only Joel had given her the chance.

"Maybe it is. Maybe it's annoying for my long-suffering husband. I don't know. But I pray hard, too," Gloria said. "And that counts for more."

Claire smiled. "*Yah*, I agree. That's where the power is, isn't it?"

That evening, after the Wassels had turned in and Aaron was tucked into his little bed with Goliath lying on the rag rug next to him, Claire went back downstairs. Aaron had left his wooden farm animals on the floor in the kitchen, and she bent down to gather them up.

Aaron loved these little animals. They'd belonged to another boy in the community of Redemption, and when he outgrew playing with them, he gave them to Aaron last year. She and Aaron had just arrived, and having something new to play with had been a welcome distraction. He still loved this play set.

The door to Joel's room opened, and she looked up to see him come hobbling out of the room in the direction of the potbellied stove. She spotted a towel on the top of the stove, warming.

Gloria's marriage advice was still trickling through her mind. Gloria and Ted had never guessed at the heartbreak they'd endure together, and yet, *Gott* had held them fast. That was the only explanation, really.

But Ted had married Gloria. That commitment counted, too.

"Are you in much pain?" Claire asked.

"I'll be okay."

It wasn't an answer. "I'll bring you more ice."

"You don't have to."

"Joel, I landed on you. I think it's the least I can do." She shot him an apologetic smile. "I do feel bad about that. I shouldn't have dragged you up onto that roof."

"You didn't drag me." His voice dropped, and he met her gaze. "Besides, if that tree were still up there, you'd lose more shingles, and it'd cause more damage."

"Very logical."

He was silent, watching her, and she dropped her gaze. She had to take control of this relationship again. She was tired of feeling tugged along with these unwelcome feelings that kept sweeping up inside her when it came to Joel. She was a grown woman and a *mamm* to boot. She needed a man who wanted commitment, and she had to stop derailing herself from getting the marriage she wanted with a man who didn't want marriage.

"All the same, I'll bring you ice." Claire adjusted her tone to something more confident. "Go on in and get comfortable in your chair."

Joel did as she told him, and Claire got more ice from the ice chest, wrapped it in a clean tea towel and went to the door of his suite. It was open, but she paused and tapped on the door all the same.

"Come in, Claire." Joel sounded like he was in pain.

She went into the room and found him in the chair angled in front of the window. His injured leg was stretched out in front of him on a footrest. He looked pale in the soft light from a dimmed lamp. The room was chilly, though, and his fire had burned down.

"Here." Claire gently laid the ice on his knee, and he caught the towel to hold it in place, his fingers brushing against hers.

"Thanks."

Claire turned to the stove and opened it, then added another two pieces of wood to the coals, nestling them in so that they quickly caught fire. She blew into the belly of the stove, and the flames grew, and when she looked back over at Joel, she found his gaze locked on her.

"I'm sure the owner will want you to keep

managing this place," he said. "You're good at this."

"I put a guest on the roof and then fell on him," she with a small smile. "If you were an *Englisher*, this might be a lawsuit."

"I'm not an *Englisher*," he replied. "Besides, I'm not really a guest, either."

"True."

He moved his foot off the footrest. "Sit down."

She looked toward the open door. Was this appropriate? Probably not. But Joel wasn't just another guest—he was right about that. She sank onto the footrest, the heat from the stove comfortably warming her back.

"This isn't as easy to handle on my own as Naomi made it look," she said quietly. "She made it all seem so effortless. It...takes more effort for me."

"I daresay it took just as much effort for her," he replied. "You make it all look easy, too."

"You're just saying that." She smiled. "Thank you, though. I really need Adel to trust me."

He leaned forward, resting his elbows on his knees. She reached toward his hurt knee and touched the bandage through his pant leg.

"Are you okay?" he asked.

"Me? I'm not the one who was injured." She dropped her hand.

"I need to know, all the same. Are you okay, Claire?"

Was she? She exhaled slowly. She was tired, and her newly arranged world had just turned upside down.

"That's what I thought," he said when she didn't answer right away. He caught her hand, and his fingers were cold from the ice pack, but he held her hand firmly, not letting go. "Claire, I don't want to be this..."

"What?" She frowned.

"Your burden."

"It's okay—"

"No." He leaned forward. "It really isn't. You don't need someone else leaning on you. You need someone to make life easier. You're already working so hard, pouring all of your energy into raising Aaron, taking care of your guests, managing a business..." He licked his lips. "Claire, I didn't want to do this to you."

"It isn't your fault, though, is it?"

"Maybe not, but I still hate it." He reached up and touched her cheek. "And I'm sorry."

"The *Englishers* think there's something between us." She smiled. She meant it as a warning—he wasn't hiding it as well as he might think. Whatever it was that had sparked between them five years ago seemed to be fighting to reignite, and it would be wise to tamp it down now.

"Maybe they're right."

Claire blinked. "You know it's more complicated."

"I know. Our situation is definitely unique," he said. "But there is something between us. There's a little someone between us. We're parents, you and I. We aren't strangers."

"No, not strangers," she said with a soft laugh.

"You loved me once," he murmured.

"You loved me, too," she countered.

"I completely adored you, Claire."

Her breath caught in her throat, and his dark gaze moved over her face. He used to say how much he loved her when they'd go for walks outside in the warm August evenings. He used to kiss her fingers and tell her that no one would ever have his heart again.

Joel leaned forward and touched her chin. She could have pulled back, stood up, done anything, but instead she found herself closing that last inch between them until she could feel his breath tickling her lips.

Joel was motionless for a moment, then he sighed as if something inside him broke, and he slid his hand behind her neck and pulled her into a kiss. Her eyes fluttered shut. The only parts of them that touched were his lips on hers and his hand on the back of her neck. His kiss was filled with longing, but she could feel his restraint, too. This wasn't a kiss from years ago. This was something new…a kiss from a man who knew the limits now. He pulled back and exhaled a shaky breath. When she opened her eyes, his were still closed.

"I've wanted to do that ever since I laid eyes on you again," he whispered, his eyes opening.

"But we can't do this, Joel," she whispered.

"I know…"

"We *really* can't!" Because if he knew her so well, he wouldn't have kissed her to begin with. "We aren't courting."

"I know." His voice firmed. "I promised myself I'd do better by you this time."

What did he mean by that? Was he hoping for another chance at a romance, or…was that a promise not to start one up? She was afraid to ask, and she stood up, attempting to put a little more distance between them. It would seem that their attraction was still there…and that could be dangerous.

"I'm going to—" she gestured toward the door "—um, I'm going to leave."

It wasn't the pithy, mature response she was hoping to give him—something that would show him just how much stronger she was now, even if she didn't feel it.

"*Yah.* Okay." Joel smiled then, his dark gaze catching hers, and her stomach flipped in response.

He was much changed from five years ago, but one thing remained the same: his ability to make her knees feel weak with one of his offhand grins. She turned and left the room, pulling the door shut behind her, and then she stopped with her hand on the knob, her heart thundering in her chest louder than the storm outside.

He'd kissed her! And it had been wonderful—and frustrating and completely wrong. She couldn't play with this.

On the other side of the door, she heard the lock click into place, and she pulled her hand off the knob as if burned. She walked quickly to the staircase and started up.

Was Joel toying with her?

If he was, she could only blame herself, because toying or not, she was playing along. Joel Beiler could only cause her difficulties. She let out a slow breath.

No more of this. And she headed upstairs to bed.

Chapter Eight

Joel lay in bed that night, his knee comfortable enough if he didn't move it. The little dawdie hus suite was cozy with the woodstove burning, and he listened to the sound of rain on the window.

He shouldn't have kissed her. He knew that, and he was already feeling bad about it, but having her so close, listening to her talk about other people's assumptions… Maybe he wanted their guesses to be true. But mostly, he'd just wanted to kiss her once more, because he'd dreamed of it for years. He used to lie in that hospital bed, thinking of her, even though he knew it was necessary to set her free. And when he saw her again standing on that porch in the rain, her blue eyes suddenly widening in recognition, he'd had to physically restrain himself from pulling her back into his arms. So the temptation had been too much, having her there, so close, smelling of lavender and baking… He'd kissed her.

And she'd kissed him back.

That fact made him smile in the darkness in spite of it all. Claire felt something for him, too. If he were a man with more to offer, that would feel like victory.

Gott, how thoughtless was that kiss? he prayed as he lay there under the thick quilt. *Lord, I wasn't trying to do wrong. But what I feel for her... It's back! Please, take away these feelings. Help me to see her as only the mother of my son—nothing more. If that is even possible...*

Because Claire was the woman he'd loved, and while he'd made mistakes, she was now also the mother of his child. *His* child. And that linked them in a profound way that he couldn't deny. He felt an urge to protect and provide for both of them. It was like that family circle had closed around his heart, even though Claire wanted nothing of the sort.

But they were a family—two people who'd made a child together, and who now needed to do what was best for that little boy. Joel had a family…and Claire wanted him to go away, and his son would be better off without a father he'd regret. But still…

He tried to unravel that knot in his mind as his breath became even and deep, and he finally fell asleep and didn't dream.

The next day, the rain stopped. The sky stayed overcast and threatening, but for the first time in days, there was no sound of rain on the roof or against the windows. There was no more thunder. And Claire's demeanor had changed, too.

At breakfast, she wouldn't meet his gaze, and she ate quickly, then left the table. When everyone had finished eating, Joel tried to talk to her in the kitchen.

"I'm cleaning, Joel."

"*Yah.* I see that. I can help you—"

"No, you need to rest. You should go to the sitting room. The light is better in front of that window. You could read."

Yah. As far from her as possible. She wasn't being very subtle.

"You're upset with me," he said quietly.

"No."

"Claire, don't lie to me."

Her face paled. "I am not a liar."

That had triggered something for her, and

he realized in a rush that he didn't know her as well as used to think he did. Their relationship had been a whirlwind romance, and then five years of silence.

"I'm not calling you a liar, I'm..." He searched around in his head for the right thing to say. "I changed things between us, didn't I?"

"*Yah.* You did. But I'm not upset with you. I'm upset with myself." She wrung out a cloth and started to wipe down a counter, her movements quick and terse.

"For letting me kiss you?" he whispered.

"*Yah.*" She wiped some crumbs into her hand and dropped them into the sink.

Seeing the regret in those blue eyes stabbed his heart. That kiss had been a relief to him, the culmination of a great deal of longing. And for her? It had been something else, it seemed. He didn't want to be her source of guilt or her deepest regret.

"I'm sorry," he said.

"Like I said, I blame myself. I'm a grown woman. I could have stopped you." She flicked the rag over the sink, then rinsed it and wrung it out again. Would she ever stop that incessant cleaning?

"Claire, I'm not some random man visiting

your establishment. You aren't having some immoral fling with a random stranger..."

"Like I did before?" She raised her glittering gaze to meet his.

The anger was back. He'd really overstepped. When he'd been a traveling farm worker and she'd been the beautiful girl he met that first service Sunday, their spark had been immediate, and he hadn't been able to take his eyes off her ever since. There had been more than one older man who'd suggested he just marry her and get it over with—the older folks had seen all the signs. But that connection between them seemed to have survived, even if she was regretting it now.

He swallowed. "Claire..."

"Joel, I know we loved each other once." Claire dried her hands slowly on a tea towel. "I know there were extenuating circumstances. I know all that...but we are still not in any position to speak about a future together, and that means that we have to be proper and modest. It's only right."

"*Yah*, I understand." Joel pushed his thumbs under his suspenders. "I'm sorry to have offended you."

He was more than sorry. He was embarrassed, too.

"I'm not..." Claire licked her lips. "I'm not really offended. I'm just... This is not easy. I have a future to think of, and Aaron needs a *daet* in his life who doesn't need to be explained, you know? You're complicated. How can he tell other boys his *daet* lives in another community and his parents aren't married? How can he see you once in a while and have that be enough? He needs a *daet* who is there every day and who teaches him things that men do. He deserves that."

Aaron deserved more than Joel could give.

"*Yah*, he does." His son deserved a better father than he was going to be—one who wouldn't make his mother look bad by association. The community had forgiven her for a youthful mistake with a terrible man who left her. But a man who came back and simply didn't marry her would change the collective view, and he knew it. "Are you going to write back to that farmer in Oregon?"

"*Yah*... I will. Soon."

"Why haven't you done it yet? You should have done it right away. I'm sure he's waiting and second-guessing everything he wrote in that letter."

He almost felt bad for the man. Almost.

"Because I—" Claire's cheeks flushed. "Because—"

"Because of me?"

"Right now, *yah*. It's because of you. Do you think any of this is easy for me? I have you back in my life after five years of trying to set you aside for good. And now you're in my home, getting to know Aaron, and… and…" She pressed her lips together.

"And kissing you."

"And kissing me!" Her blue eyes flashed fire. "That isn't fair."

"Then forget the kiss."

"As easily as that?" She shot him an annoyed look.

Had it been so memorable for her? He'd thought it was only him who'd be tucking that memory into a sacred little spot in his heart.

"You *can* just forget about that, you know," he said. "I won't be hurt. I take full responsibility for it."

At least he wouldn't tell her that he was hurt. She rolled her eyes.

"You don't just kiss a woman like that and expect her to be able to toss it aside, Joel. I'm not the kind of woman who goes around kissing men on a regular basis. You're—" The color in her face deepened. "You're the only man I've ever kissed."

"*Yah?*" He caught her hand, and she tugged her fingers free.

"*Yah.*" She looked up at him again. "So cut it out."

"Okay. I will. That's a promise."

"And I'm going to write to that farmer," she said, her tone almost accusing.

"Good. You should, if that's what you want."

"I'm going to talk seriously about marriage."

"I understand."

Claire nodded resolutely, and he had a feeling she was trying to summon up her own courage to do it, because the look in her eyes wasn't matching the confidence of her words. She should do just that, though. And he shouldn't be holding her back.

Joel's knee ached the more time he spent standing up, and he hobbled over to a kitchen chair and sank into it. Heat from the potbellied stove did help a little bit, and he stretched his leg out toward it.

"Can I go to out to play?" Aaron pleaded from where he sat by the window.

"No, Aaron," Claire said. "It's too dangerous out there. We'll wait until the water goes down."

"But I want to play in the water!" He stuck out his lower lip. "I want to float a boat!"

"Aaron, I said no."

Claire was getting to the end of her patience, and Joel looked over at the little wooden farm Aaron had spread out on the floor next to the table. Claire wanted her son to learn things from men, and while another man would be the *daet* Aaron could be proud of, maybe Joel could offer something.

In the wood box, he spotted a couple of small chunks of cut wood.

"Aaron, do you want more cows for your farm?" Joel asked.

"More cows?" Aaron looked over, eyes glistening with interest.

"I can show you how to make some." He pulled his pocketknife out. "Get me some wood over there…"

He could do this still, couldn't he? His left hand wasn't as strong as it used to be, and he hadn't actually whittled since before the stroke. He had a sudden surge of misgiving, but Aaron was already poking around in the wood box, Goliath next to him.

The dog wandered away from Aaron's side and came over to where Joel sat. Without thinking, Joel reached out and stroked the dog's head. Goliath let him pet him, sidling a little closer so Joel could reach better.

"Hey." Joel looked down at the dog. "I'm not so bad, huh?"

"He likes you now." Aaron emerged with some pieces of wood, and he brought them over to Joel's lap.

Joel chose a piece of wood that was small enough to shape. "Do you see the cow in this wood?"

Aaron shook his head.

"Listen..." Joel held it close to Aaron's ear, and then made a soft mooing sound. Aaron started to laugh, and Joel grinned. "It's in there. This curve? That's the top of the cow's head. We just have to get to it. I'll show you."

He started to take off curls of fragrant wood with his pocketknife, and as he whittled, Aaron pulled a chair up next to him to watch. His left hand was cooperating today, it seemed. It wasn't as strong, so Joel used his knee for leverage as he worked.

"You can grow your herd this way," Joel said. "Your cows can have calves. You could even start a little herd of pigs, if you figured out how to make them."

"Could I make them?" Aaron looked up at him in interest.

"*Yah.* I'll show you. Come here. You want to try?"

Claire cleared her throat, and Joel looked over his shoulder at her. Right—this wasn't his call to make.

"I was whittling at his age," Joel explained.

"That's a sharp knife," she said.

Was that a comment on his current abilities?

"How about you, Ted? When did you start sharpening sticks?" Joel asked.

"Oh...close to that age," Ted agreed.

Claire sighed. "All right. But you keep an eye on him."

"You want to try?" Joel asked.

Aaron nodded eagerly.

"Okay, so come stand here." Joel brought his son between his knees. "And you'll hold on to the knife nice and tightly, okay? And you always cut away from you. Always. Got it?"

Aaron was an eager learner, but he tended to grip the knife and the wood so tightly that Joel could hardly guide him. So they'd stop, and Joel would go over it again, and ever so slowly, Aaron got the hang of it.

"There you go," Joel said. "Now let me take over for a bit, because I'm going to shape this part that's going to be his back. Like this—"

Joel drew with the tip of the knife to show Aaron how it would look.

"Okay." Aaron relinquished his position and crawled up on the chair next to him again so he could watch.

Joel's hand didn't respond as well as it should, which meant it was better for Aaron to step back anyway. If that had been Claire's worry, perhaps it was more founded than he'd previously thought. If Joel had better control of his fingers on his left hand, he'd be able to add all sorts of detail, like horns, a tail, eyes…but what he'd manage with his current clumsy ability would be a piece of wood roughly the same shape as a cow. It was like the image of himself in his head—so much different from reality.

He noticed Claire from the corner of his eye, watching him. Her expression had softened, tenderness shining in her blue eyes, and an overwhelming surge of longing forced him to focus on the wood, and only the wood.

She wanted the Oregon farmer. Good. She *should* write to him.

"My *daet* taught me how to whittle," Joel said to Aaron.

It was one of the few positive memories he had with his father. It was before the biggest stroke that had stolen his father's fine motor skills and his happiness all in one blow. It was when his father had a bit of a limp and some slurring speech but otherwise was okay.

"What did you make with your *daet*?" Aaron asked.

"We whittled a wooden spoon for my *mamm*." Joel's had been lopsided and crooked, but his mother had used it that very day for mixing up a pitcher of lemonade.

"Did you ever make a wooden farm?" Aaron asked hopefully.

"I wish I'd thought of it," Joel replied. "But no. I did make a buggy once."

"Out of wood?" Aaron brightened.

"It was a hunk of wood that almost looked like a buggy already," Joel said. "That's the secret. You decide what you're going to make after looking at the wood."

He had to see what was possible, what would emerge from the wood most naturally. He glanced over his shoulder toward Claire, and she was still watching them. He should take the same advice with her. Joel knew what was possible between them, and he needed to let this misplaced hope that had been building inside him go.

Joel swallowed and put his attention back

into the whittling. The problem was, ever since he'd first seen her, he'd been powerless to stop his feelings for Claire. She was special—there was no getting around it. She was the only woman to capture his heart like that, and there had never been another.

A cell phone rang—a strange sound in an Amish house—and he turned again to see Gloria pick a phone up from the counter.

"It's Ashley!" She picked up the call. "Hi, sweetheart… Yes, we're fine, but I have hardly any battery left, so… The rain has stopped… No, no, dear. Your father and I are just fine… We had that extra phone charging battery pack in the car that you gave us. I'm so glad you thought of it."

Joel glanced at Ted.

"Our daughter," Ted said. "She's been worried about us, since this was only supposed to be an afternoon trip. We've been texting."

Goliath nudged Aaron's hand, and the boy wrapped an arm around the dog's neck. Aaron's attention was fixed on Joel's hands as he worked, and somehow Joel felt like his paltry efforts that looked mostly like a cow as he shaved away the wood were more than that. This was a memory with his son…even if Aaron might never know it this side of eternity.

"I don't want to give Goliath back," Aaron said softly.

"It's going to be hard, isn't it?" Joel patted his shoulder.

Aaron nodded. "I love him."

"You know, a lot of times, the right thing to do is the hard thing," Joel said. "That's what separates real men from the ones who aren't worthy."

"What does?"

"Doing the hardest thing because it's right. A lesser man would take the easy route. A real man—he looks at things as they are. He doesn't pretend they are any different. And he knows what he has to do."

"I don't want to be a man yet." Aaron's lips trembled. "I want to be a boy."

"Well, I can understand that," Joel agreed. "But we can't tell when the test will come. We just have to straighten our shoulders and do the right thing."

Like Joel was going to do. He'd hand over that money to Claire, and he'd walk away. If he were still the man he used to be, he'd stay and sweep her off her feet. He'd raise his son and build them a house. He'd support them and provide. But he couldn't do that now, and staying here would only put more burden onto

Claire's shoulders…and ruin her chances at a proper marriage.

Joel was facing the truth of it.

"So I should be strong and give Goliath back?" Aaron's question tugged Joel's attention back.

"*Yah.* You'll feel better once you've done the right thing. I promise."

And for a little boy who gave a dog back to its rightful owners, he might. He'd be sad, but he'd know in his young heart that he'd done the right thing. For Joel, however, doing the right thing here with Claire wasn't going to make him feel better. In fact, he'd carry the burden of this loss for the rest of his days.

Claire came over behind him, and he felt the touch of her apron against the back of his shoulder as she looked down at his whittling. His breath caught, and he could smell that unique scent that was hers—that hint of lavender. Where did it come from—soap, maybe? It was new, though, not a scent from years ago. This was part of the woman she was now, and it was an aroma that would follow him in his memories, he was sure.

"You'll have a new cow, Aaron," Claire said with a smile in her voice. "Isn't that great?"

Ted reached over and took the piece of wood from Joel's hands.

"Looks good," he said. "Very nice. This is definitely looking bovine already."

Behind them Gloria was chatting with her daughter, and then her voice suddenly stopped. Joel turned to see her standing there with the cell phone in her hand and tears welling in her eyes.

"Gloria? Honey?" Ted started to stand up.

Gloria clamped a hand over her mouth, and her shoulders shook. Claire hurried over to her, and Ted blindly shoved the piece of wood back into Joel's hand and stood up, all in one movement.

"My phone is dead." Gloria sniffled. "And… and I couldn't tell Ashley what I wanted to, and…"

Ted crossed the room and pulled his wife into his arms. She leaned her head against his chest, and for a moment, she seemed silent. Then Joel heard her soft sobs. Ted rested his cheek against her head, and when he looked over at Joel, Joel dropped his gaze.

This was a private moment between a husband and a wife, and he felt Claire's hand on his shoulder. He reached up and caught her fingers in his. Joel felt his own throat tighten, but it was more than sympathy for Gloria's obvious heartbreak that seemed like it had little to do with a dead battery.

The lump in Joel's throat came with the realization that he'd never be the man to hold Claire like that. He tightened his grip on her hand. He'd never be her hero, her husband, her rock when she needed someone to cry on. That felt wrong on a heart level. It should be him…always him.

"It's okay, Gloria," Ted said softly. "I know. I know…"

When Joel looked at him again, Ted added, "It's a tough time of year."

And that covered it. Gloria had been holding it all together, and her grief had finally broken through. Gloria had lost a son.

Joel reached over and put his other hand on Aaron's curly head. Loss could come in so many different forms, and he felt his own sadness rising up. Would he see his son again? Would Aaron ever know that his real *daet* had loved him?

Claire slipped her hand free of his grip, and he let her go. Joel's grief would have to wait until he was home and he could bow under the weight of it alone.

Chapter Nine

Claire went back into the kitchen, and she looked over her shoulder as Ted and Gloria quietly went upstairs. They'd want privacy at a time like this, and she could understand all too well. Her hand was still warm from where Joel had touched her, and she felt silly all over again.

She'd just finished telling Joel that she fully intended to answer that letter, and in an emotionally fraught moment, she'd reached out to him. It had been alarmingly instinctive, too. She had to stop this!

Would a husband understand this strange connection she had with the father of her son? No, he wouldn't. It would be inappropriate, and she'd be wholeheartedly in the wrong. She needed to curb it now.

"Why is she crying?" Aaron's little voice rang through the room. Claire winced, wishing he'd keep his voice down, but it wasn't his fault.

"She's very sad," Claire replied.

"Why?"

Claire didn't want to put that kind of burden onto his small shoulders. "It's something private, sweetheart. She'll be okay. She has her husband to help her."

Joel caught her gaze then, and her heart skipped a beat. Yes, she'd heard it when it came out of her mouth, too—Gloria would be okay because of her husband. Who would make things okay for Claire? Would it be a farmer from Oregon or perhaps a widower closer to home? She'd been strong for a long time, and she was starting to long for that shoulder to lean on.

That letter lay on her dresser upstairs, but Claire didn't have it in her to talk about basket weaving or about growing herbs or even about raising her son. She had no more emotional energy to tell him about her worries that a stepfather might be too harsh, or to assure him that she would do her best to make all the foods that her new husband loved most.

You've got to sell yourself a little, Adel had

told her when she handed her the envelope, and Claire knew she should do just that. She should put her best foot forward and show that she would be a good woman to marry.

She should…

But her heart was full of memories from five years ago, and her lips were still tingling from a kiss much more recent. And she'd been angry, because it wasn't fair for Joel to do this to her! How on earth was she supposed to move on with her life when Joel was upending it all over again?

So what would she say mattered most to her in a husband when she finally did answer that letter? Kindness—both to her son, and to her. And love—as much as he could summon up for a virtual stranger.

That was the catch. It was awfully hard to marry a man she wasn't in love with when she knew what that kind of love felt like. Even if it had stung her. Her friend Naomi had balked at an arranged marriage for that exact reason. She'd wanted love—the real, unfiltered, head-over-heels kind of love. That was hard to demand. It either existed or it didn't, but Claire had seen it spring up for Naomi. Claire had even sent up a vulnerable little prayer that *Gott* might give her the same. And this resurgence of emotion for Joel Beiler felt like cruelty. She needed love with an appropriate man, not to relive this heartbreak all over again!

An hour later, Ted came back downstairs, and Claire shot him a sympathetic smile from where she stood by the stove, pouring freshly boiled water into a teapot.

"Everything okay?" she asked.

"Yes. It's just a tough time."

"Do you think she might like a hot cup of tea?" Claire put the lid on the pot.

"Actually, I think she would."

"I'll bring it up to her," Claire said. "I've got some sandwiches made, if you'd like something to eat."

Claire poured a cup of tea, added sugar and slipped past the men. In the Amish world, women took care of each other in a rather special way. Husbands were important, as were children and extended family, but women circled around when another sister needed support. A husband was important, but he couldn't be everything.

Claire tapped on the Wassels' door.

"Come in." Gloria sounded a little surprised, and when Claire opened the door, she found Gloria quickly wiping her face. "I'm sorry about this, Claire. I didn't mean to just break down like that."

"No apologies necessary," Claire said, coming inside. She handed Gloria the cup of tea. "I find something hot and sweet helps."

"Thank you." She accepted it and took a sip.

Claire sat down on the easy chair next to the window, angling her knees toward Gloria, who sat on the edge of the bed.

"My grandmother told me something years ago," Claire said. "She said a husband is a gift from *Gott*, but a circle of praying sisters keeps a woman on her feet."

Gloria blinked at her.

"We all need each other," Claire said.

"I'm not despairing, if that's what you think." Gloria took a sip of her tea. "I know I'll see Royden again. I know he's with God, and he's the safest he's ever been. I know this life is just a drop in the bucket of eternity, and I will have the rest of time with my son at my side. I know all of that..."

"But right now, you miss him," Claire whispered.

"Yeah, that covers it." Gloria gave her a wobbly smile. "I suppose basket weaving wasn't going to make me forget it."

For a few minutes, they talked about Gloria's son, about what a sweet baby he'd been, what a gallant young man... They talked about what it felt like for a mother to be without her child in the world and how that unique and stabbing grief never really went away.

"We weren't created for this," Gloria said softly. "We weren't meant to ever know what loss felt like. So it can break us, if God doesn't hold us together."

Grief could indeed break a woman or, perhaps even worse, harden her into an angry, bitter version of herself. Claire was a little afraid that the only way to get over Joel was going to be to grow harder and more callused.

"How are things with Joel?" Gloria asked. "It's okay to change the subject. I need the distraction."

"Nothing has changed."

"So he's in love with you, and you're rebuffing him?"

"I don't trust that he's in love with me," Claire replied. "It's emotionally complicated—that's all. He's Aaron's father." Claire licked her lips. "If I'm going to tell you the whole story, I'd better include that."

"I know," Gloria said. "Ted told me. He and Joel were talking, so I didn't actually guess all of this. But Ted and I could tell there was a special connection between the two of you. And a little boy—he's a pretty special connection."

"Yes, it is special, and it complicates feelings. He's discovered that he's a father. I imagine that might cloud his reasoning a bit."

"I don't think it's unreasonable for him to have feelings for you," Gloria said.

"Maybe not, but he's already decided he doesn't want marriage. He's sick, you see, and he's determined to do this on his own." She paused. "He left me when he got sick five years ago, and he doesn't want to be a burden on a wife. And even though he's Aaron's father, I don't think I should have to talk a man into staying. If he doesn't want me there with him during his hard times, then lifelong vows are not for us. I know you probably think I shouldn't be so picky, but—"

"I never said that," Gloria cut in. "I agree with you, Claire. If he doesn't want marriage, he doesn't want it. Men can't be reformed so easily. You're right to stand by your principles."

"Thank you," Claire said, the fight going out of her.

"But I understand how important marriage

is to a woman," Gloria said. "Maybe even more so in your culture."

"It is rather important," Claire agreed. "Our faith, our church, our way of life is all centered around marriage and children. When a woman dies and is buried, she's dressed in her wedding clothes one last time."

"That's beautiful," Gloria murmured.

"If you've been married to a man who loved you, then yes," Claire agreed. "If you were single…it's one last reminder to everyone that you didn't have a family."

The women were silent for a few beats, and Claire looked outside at the gray, rainy day. When would this end? When would her personal storms pass? She could see a few rays of sunlight slanting down a mile or so away. So this rainstorm would end soon.

"There's always comfort in Easter," Gloria said quietly.

"*Yah*." A hope for Heaven. A hope for salvation. Was that the best that Claire could put her hope in here in her earthly life—the hereafter?

"Marriage isn't everything." Gloria put the teacup down on the bedside table.

"I know."

"I'm serious. I'm thinking specifically of

the single women who were with Jesus—Mary Magdalene or Martha and Mary, the sisters of Lazarus. Those were women who are remembered by name—not because of their husbands or children, but because of their place in God's story. So many women slipped through the cracks of history, even the women married to powerful men, but not *those* women. And all three of those women appear to have been both single and childless. And we remember them by name."

"I'd never thought of it that way."

"Well, maybe you should start," Gloria said seriously. "Jesus had a special place in His heart for those women, and their value had nothing to do with husbands or families. I like to think that He eventually brought them the desires of their hearts—possibly husbands and children, if that was what they wanted."

"Do you think? It's not in the Bible, though."

"It isn't, but sometimes I look at those stories and wonder what happened afterward. Is our God limited?"

"No," Claire whispered. "Not one bit."

"Well, then my faith allows for a happily-ever-after for every single one of them."

Gloria was right. *Gott* was not limited or shortsighted or taken by surprise.

Claire smiled and reached out, squeezing Gloria's hand. "You're quite wonderful, Gloria."

"So are you, Claire." Gloria squeezed her hand back. "And never forget it, okay? I don't know what will happen with Aaron's dad, but I do know that God is still working."

"He's still working," she echoed softly.

Perhaps Claire would end up with her own story of heartbreak and resurrection, where *Gott* helped her to put her past behind her and to step forward into a new and joyful future. Maybe this would be her painful tale to tell, but one that would encourage another young woman coming up behind. She'd just have to trust *Gott* that there was a beautiful, satisfying, fulfilling life after Joel.

Her faith would have to be stronger than her heartache.

Joel made himself comfortable in an easy chair in the sitting room, Ted across from him with a book in his lap. But Ted's gaze wasn't on the page. It was directed out the window. Rays of golden sunlight slanted down from holes torn in the cloudy sky. The bad weather was breaking up. This was good news—no storm lasted forever. But it also meant that Joel would be able to leave. He'd be obligated to.

Would Claire ever tell Aaron that he'd met his father? A lump tightened his throat.

"It's like a river out there," Ted said from where he stood at the window.

"*Yah.* It's pretty bad. But the rain's stopped. You'd be surprised how fast the land can drain once that happens."

"There's got to be a life lesson in there somewhere, huh?" Ted smiled ruefully.

"There has to be." But Joel's heart felt heavy all the same.

For most people's lives, there probably was a lesson about hard times passing and sunny days returning again. But some people, like Joel, had a lifelong illness to contend with. It wouldn't get easier for him.

He turned his attention to his son's play with his toy farm. Aaron leaned over the wooden barn, adding the newly whittled cow to his herd. The boy talked to himself as he arranged his cattle and then happily counted them for the umpteenth time.

"Can we make more?" Aaron asked, sitting up on his haunches.

"*Yah*, but it will have to be later." Joel's bad hand was sore, and his fingers felt weaker for the exercise.

"I want more cows," Aaron said. "Maybe some baby cows?"

"If I'm here." Joel rubbed the palm of his hand, pushing his thumb into the flesh.

"Are you going away soon?"

"Well, I was just passing through, Aaron. The storm kept me here. I'll have to go back home."

"Where do you live?"

"Ohio."

"Is it nice in Ohio?"

"It's very nice." Joel smiled. "Maybe you'll see Ohio one day."

Maybe he'd visit. Maybe Claire would finally tell Aaron who he was and the boy would want to see where his *daet* lived, meet his *mammi* and his other aunts and uncles…

"*Yah*, maybe!" But Aaron's attention was on the farm. To Aaron, Joel was just a passing guest. Wasn't there some piece of the boy that would recognize his real father—some God-given sense inside him?

Goliath wandered over to Aaron's farm set and sniffed at a wooden fence that tipped over with a clatter.

"Goliath, you can't do that." Aaron pushed the dog back. Goliath cooperatively sat down, but his nose started to descend again as soon as Aaron went back to his play. "Goliath!"

Goliath got up and padded over to the front door, then looked back meaningfully.

"I think he needs to go out," Ted said. "There's not a lot of grass left for him to do his business."

Aaron looked up. "Do you need to go out, Goliath?"

The dog sat down at the door and woofed softly. Aaron got up and went over to the door. He pulled it open and Goliath trotted out. Aaron leaned against the door frame, watching. Joel could see the dog from the window, nosing around the edge of a virtual lake, sniffing. He took a step into the water.

"Goliath, you'll get dirty!" Aaron hollered.

The dog took another step, and then another, and then, without any further hesitation, he pushed himself down into the water and started to paddle for the other side.

"That's deeper than I thought!" Joel stood up. His knee ached in protest, and he hobbled closer to the window.

"Goliath!" Aaron hollered, annoyed. "You will be very, very dirty now!"

Ted stood up, too, and they both looked at the dog, paddling across the lake toward higher ground beyond. Was the dog going to find home? Maybe he wasn't as lost as they all seemed to think. It was then that Joel spotted Aaron wading into the water after the dog, and Joel's heart thudded to a stop.

"Aaron!" He limped to the open door. "Aaron, get back here!"

"I'm just going to get my dog!" Aaron yelled over his shoulder. "Don't worry! I can do it!"

Ted leaned closer to the window. "How deep is that?"

There was a dangerous-looking swirl of muddy water about a yard ahead of the boy, and if the water was at its deepest, it would be okay, but every step brought the muddy water higher up Aaron's legs, soaking his pants.

"Aaron, I want you to come back *now*," he ordered. There was authority in his voice—the kind that came from rising anxiety for his son's safety.

"It's not too deep." Aaron's piping voice filtered through the sound of draining water. "I can get him."

Joel wasn't someone for Aaron to obey. Joel was just a guest passing through. There was no reason for Aaron to jump and do as he was told by a relative stranger, was there? Aaron waded farther, the water past his waist now, and then he stepped into a current of water leading farther down, draining off somewhere that Joel couldn't see, and the boy's legs seemed to go out from under him. He went down with hardly a splash and disappeared under the water.

Joel launched himself out the house, limping as fast as he could go, pushing himself forward with his good leg and barely catching himself with his bad one. Pain shot up his knee, but he kept moving. He splashed into the water just as Aaron came up coughing, and he shot out a hand, latching onto Aaron's shirt with an iron grip. Joel hauled the boy out of the water and tossed him over his shoulder, then turned back toward the house.

In the upstairs window, he saw Claire's white face, then she disappeared. Joel limped toward the door, and he put Aaron down on the step. The boy coughed once more and tried to head past Joel outside again.

"Goliath!" Aaron called.

The dog had clambered up on the higher ground and barked back at them.

"No!" Joel said. "Aaron, come on! You could have drowned!"

"But Goliath has to come back!" Aaron pleaded as Joel nudged him back inside.

Claire's footsteps came drumming down the stairs, and when she emerged into the living room, her hair had come loose from her *kapp* and her face was ashen.

"Aaron!" She ran up to the boy and wrapped her arms around him in a fierce hug, then pulled back and ran her hands over his head and wet hair. There was a damp, muddy smear left on the front of her dress. "Are you okay?"

"*Yah*, I'm fine. I just got dunked," he said.

"In runoff water," Joel said.

"But *Mamm*, Goliath is out there!" Aaron pleaded.

"I'll get him," Joel said, and he hobbled to the door. The dog was sniffing around on the other side of the muddy lake, and he didn't look up when Joel whistled.

"Goliath!" Aaron called. "Come back!"

"Goliath!" Joel called, louder and more commanding than the boy could manage, but the dog ignored them both, continuing his sniffing.

"I'm just going to—" Aaron started.

"All right, that's quite enough!" Claire

stood up, and Joel and Aaron both froze and looked over at her. Ted, from over by the window was watching Claire, too, a look of mild surprise on his face.

"Aaron, you sit down *right now* and do as you're told," Claire snapped. "You were told over and over again to get out of that water and come inside, and you didn't listen!"

Aaron looked from his mother then over to Joel with a perplexed look on his face. Obviously listening to Joel made very little sense in his young mind. Who was Joel to them?

"You should be thankful that Joel bothered himself to go out after you!" Claire went on. "If you get a horrible cough from all that muddy water in your lungs, you only have yourself to blame, young man! I want you to remember that. Floodwater is full of all sorts of junk, and you don't go swimming in it!"

"I didn't mean to go swimming, I was going to get Goliath. It wasn't on purpose!"

"Did I ask?" Claire, apparently, was in no mood, and her eyes flashed in fury.

"But *Mamm*—" Aaron started, and Claire held up a single finger, pinning her son back into his seat with a stern look.

"Sit. Still." Claire whirled around and marched past Joel and Ted to the door. She put two fingers in her mouth, let out a piercing whistle and shouted, "Ollie! Come!"

The authority in her voice sent a shiver down Joel's spine, and the dog turned, looked at Claire and then plunged back into the water, paddling obediently toward them. When the dog arrived at the door, he gave a mighty shake that sprayed everything around him in a fine mist of water, then padded docilely back inside. Claire wiped the sprayed water from her face with the edge of her apron, shut the door, closed her eyes and inhaled a slow, deep breath. Joel had never seen this side of Claire before—certainly not when he'd been falling for her the first time. Maybe this was the kind of authority that came with motherhood, but this home was well in hand with Claire running it. Claire opened her eyes and pasted a sweet smile on her face.

"I apologize for the drama, Ted," Claire said. "I'm going to put on some tea soon, so feel free to go get a muffin or a pastry from the kitchen." Then she turned to Joel, that no-nonsense look cracking for just a moment. "Thank you for getting him." Tears suddenly misted her eyes, and she blinked them back. "I mean it."

"Of course I would, Claire," he said in

Pennsylvania Dutch, his whole heart in the ordinary words. But he meant it with every fiber of his being. Of course he'd go after his son. When he'd seen Aaron go down, he'd known in that moment that he'd do absolutely anything for his son, and he wasn't coming back without him. Clare's gaze moved down to his muddy pants, and he looked down at a streak of dirty water across the front of his shirt.

"Goliath..." Aaron said sadly, and the dog padded up to him. "You smell terrible, Goliath." Aaron looked mournfully up at his mother. "You called him the wrong name, *Mamm*."

"I called him the right name, son," Claire said. "His name is Ollie, and he belongs to another family."

"You don't know that he's the right dog!" Aaron said. "Maybe he's a different one!"

"He came when I called him Ollie, didn't he?"

"You sounded pretty scary," Aaron said. "I don't think he was listening to his name. He was listening to how mad you were."

Joel chuckled at that, and Claire shot him an annoyed look.

"I wouldn't say scary," Joel amended. "But you were certainly impressive."

Claire rolled her eyes and turned back to her son.

"From now on, you are to call him by his real name," Claire said. "There's no use pretending otherwise. We didn't know whose he was when we found him, but now we do. Okay? Now that we know, that changes things."

Knowledge changed a lot of things—for Joel, too.

"Now, you march upstairs and start the bathwater," Claire said. "You need a very thorough bath, or you'll smell as bad as the dog." Her face softened. "And that's pretty bad right now."

"Yah, Mamm."

Aaron headed in the direction of the stairs, and Ted slipped past the boy, out into the kitchen. Claire followed them both, leaving Joel alone in the sitting room. After a moment, Claire returned with an old towel.

"Ollie, come here." She sat on the edge of the couch. The dog went over, and she shook out the towel and started to rub him dry.

All was in order again. Everyone was doing what they needed to do. The squeal of pipes announced that the bathwater had been turned on. Claire rubbed the dog's fur with firm strokes.

Claire was very well in control here, and as much as Joel wanted to help—as much as he had helped when he'd fished his son out of the water—he wasn't really needed. Claire was authority enough for their son, and within five minutes of her simply taking control of a situation, it was resolved, smoothed over and the family set right.

Claire finished with the dog and set the wet towel in her lap. She looked up at Joel.

"You're wet, too," she said. "I can get you a washbasin since Aaron's in the tub. And if you give me your clothes, I'll put them through the wringer washer."

"I'm fine." He shifted his weight to his good leg.

"It won't take long. I was going to wash Ted's clothes anyway. I'll add yours in."

She was back in control, and he was just another guest whose comfort she'd see to.

"You have this place under control, don't you?"

"I don't always feel like it."

"I just watched you pull everything together in two minutes flat."

Her face pinked. "I'm embarrassed. A woman doesn't normally show that side of things to—" She stopped.

"To guests," he said quietly.

She dropped her gaze.

"Claire, you're ready to run this place. You can't control the storms that come, but you have this place well in hand. I think you should just tell the owner what you want. Stop worrying that you're not ready or that she won't see it. From what I saw today, you're more than ready."

"Thank you." She eyed him for a moment. "Do you mean it?"

"I really do."

She smiled. "Well, that makes me feel better."

Claire didn't need anyone else's help running this bed-and-breakfast, and she didn't need his input around here, either. Aaron was doing just fine being raised by his loving, devoted mother. No matter how much Joel wanted to make Claire's life easier, the answer had been his first instinct from the start—that inheritance.

She didn't need him in the way he seemed to need her in this moment—on a heart level that he kept trying to soothe with halfway solutions. But halfway wasn't going to be enough for her—nor should it be.

"I'm going to go check on Aaron." Claire

shook out her dress with a wince. “I’m a mess.”

She headed off toward the staircase, and he watched her go with a heaviness in his heart. He’d fallen in love with her again. When would he learn?

Chapter Ten

Claire poked her head into the bathroom. Aaron was in the tub, the water running and a thick bar of white soap in one hand. He looked cheery, as if he hadn't just almost drowned. Watching from that upstairs window, she'd never felt more helpless in her life as when she saw her son disappear under that murky water.

Joel had saved him—literally! If he hadn't been there to fish Aaron out, who knew what might have happened? *Gott* had guided his hands for sure and certain, and no one could ever convince her otherwise.

"Here." Claire took a washcloth and rubbed a generous amount of soap into it. "Now wash your face. We're going to do your hair, as well. You're a very muddy boy."

"Where's Goliath?"

"Sweetie, I know you love him, but his name is Ollie. Okay?"

"But where is he?"

"Downstairs by the stove to dry off the rest of the way. I toweled him down, and I'm pretty sure Ted and Gloria are letting him eat table scraps."

"He likes that."

"*Yah*, he does." She washed his face and used a cup to wet down his already-wet hair, and she added a dollop of shampoo, working it into a lather through his fine hair.

"Close your eyes." She took a cupful of water and started to rinse it out.

"Sweetie," Claire said as she worked. "Ollie is probably very thankful that he found you when he did. He was all alone, very hungry and didn't know how to find his home. Sometimes *Gott* lets us be a helper. This time, *Gott* let you be Ollie's comfort until we could find his family for him. I know it's sad to say goodbye to him, but you gave Ollie a few weeks of love when he needed it most."

"I do love him." Aaron plugged his nose as water dripped down his face. She wiped his eyes with the washcloth.

"And you've taken very good care of him,

son. I think you've taken such good care of him that you've proven you're old enough to get a puppy of your own."

"Really?" Aaron's blue eyes lit up.

"*Yah*, really. But only after we've brought Ollie to his family where he belongs. And then we can look around for a puppy."

It was the best that Claire could do.

"There. Your hair is done. Now, you use lots of soap on the rest of you, son. You're filthy."

"I will." Aaron shot her a grin. "Lots and lots."

That evening, the wind started. Wind was welcome, as it would carry away a lot of the moisture and dry up the rivers of water flowing over their property. It howled and moaned around the house, like some sort of heartbroken animal looking for somewhere to rest, and Claire could almost feel her heart following after that mournful wind in spite of herself.

What was it that drew lonely, hurting people to her door? The Wassels were not the first couple to come here who'd been in search of healing. There had been other *Englishers* who'd brought their broken hearts to this bed-and-breakfast, and even that poor, lost German shepherd had found his place to rest here with them until he could go home. She and Aaron had become a sort of safe harbor for every living creature here.

Including Joel. And that thought made her breath catch. He'd come here just as broken as anyone else—in body and in spirit. He'd come here looking for answers, forgiveness, some sort of peace that she couldn't provide. And yet here he was, a part of the imperfect mix that *Gott* had tossed together for one long, isolating storm. What had *Gott* been doing here?

She'd been able to forget about Joel—most of the time—and now she found her heart a tender, aching mess all over again. Joel was going back to his life in Ohio, far away from here. Joel was the father of her son, and the source of the most painful lesson of her life, but a lesson that hadn't been lost on her: people could say beautiful things, and they could even want them to be true, but it didn't mean they had the character to back them up. Actions were what proved a man.

Why did you bring him here, Gott? she prayed. *What am I supposed to learn that I didn't know before?*

Because she knew that *Gott* wasn't wasteful. There was a purpose in everything, including Joel's arrival. She just couldn't see it.

After dinner, Claire headed to the mudroom to put on her work boots and coat, and Joel limped after her.

"I'll help with chores," he said.

She met his gaze, about to answer, when he added, "I'll be going home soon, Claire. This is my last chance to help you out. Let me do this."

She'd meant to have some time in prayer to get some balance back, but looking up into Joel's warm gaze, she didn't have the strength to turn him down. She didn't want to need Joel. She didn't want to miss him when he was gone, either. She didn't want to be feeling this crush of emotion about him all over again, either.

Claire nodded. "*Yah*. Okay."

They headed out into the driving wind, and she pushed the screen door shut after the door to make sure it wouldn't tear off its hinges in this gale. They put their heads down and made their way out to the stable. She had to slow down so that Joel could keep up, but she tried not to make it obvious.

She made it to the stable door before him and turned and waited until he caught up.

"It's hard to catch you alone with the house so full." Joel pulled open the door for her to go inside first.

"Were you trying to?"

Joel pulled the door firmly shut behind them, and Claire lit the kerosene lantern, the warm light splashing over the shuffling horses. The wind was making them uneasy, it seemed.

"*Yah*, I was. As soon as I can get a buggy through that water, I'm heading out. I needed to see you alone before I go."

"It might take a while for everything to dry out." She forced a smile, but it felt tight on her lips. Was she hoping his departure would take longer? Maybe.

"This wind will do its job," he said. "You don't want me to go?"

"I didn't say that. I just—" She didn't know what she was trying to say. A few days ago, she'd had a vision of what her life could be, and now Joel had obliterated that.

Claire opened the first stall and led the horse into an open space with oats to occupy him. She grabbed the shovel, but Joel put his hand on top of it, stopping her.

"Do you want me to go?" His dark gaze caught hers.

"Yes!"

He released the shovel and she went over to the stall to begin mucking it out. Joel brought the wheelbarrow over, and he leaned against the rail, his dark gaze pinned on her.

"I mean, I—" She stopped, the shovel clanking against the cement floor, and emotion choked her voice. "I just want to stop feeling like this, Joel."

"Like what? Have I done something?"

"I had everything under control." She started to shovel soiled hay into the wheelbarrow. "I had a way to provide for my little boy, I had a new community that was finally accepting me, I had friends and I even had some hope that I might be able to get married—something I didn't think would ever happen for me after having Aaron outside wedlock."

"You were happy before I showed up."

"I was *almost* happy!" she countered. "I was *this close* to being happy." She lifted two fingers to demonstrate. "I had happiness close enough that I could see getting there. And then, yes, you showed up!"

"And I ruin your happiness." His expression closed off. She'd hurt him, but now wasn't the time for polite banter. Now was the time for honesty.

"*Yah!*" She shook her head. "Because now, some farmer in Oregon isn't going to be enough, is he? And just having a way to make sure my son stays fed isn't going to feel like the personal success that it did a few days ago. None of this will be enough anymore."

"Because of me..."

"*Yah!* Because of you." She whirled around to face him. "Because you reminded me of things I felt five years ago that made me feel more alive than I've ever felt in my entire life." She leaned the shovel against the rail. "And maybe I have no business remembering that. You were my greatest mistake, Joel. Do you realize that? When you swept me off my feet, my life changed forever. I became a single mother, and all my hopes for a future happening in the right order were *gone*." Her hands were trembling with the strength of her emotions. "I used to dream of falling in love just like we did, Joel...but instead of being abandoned by the man who claimed to love me, a *wedding* would have come next. And then after the wedding, after a suitable amount of time, I'd discover I was pregnant, and me and my *mamm* and my sisters would all sit down together and we'd start making little baby clothes." She dashed an errant tear off her cheek. "And then, after that baby, another one and another. And my husband would be so happy and proud, and we'd be *a family.* That was the future I dreamed of."

"Claire—" He reached for her hand and squeezed it in his strong grip. "I know I did you wrong. I know that—"

"Oh, I don't blame you for that entirely, because I made a choice, too." She pulled her hand back. "I fully accept that the mistake was mine, and the consequences are mine, as well. A man never bears the same weight of blame as the woman, of course. Because we give birth to the baby and raise him and love him. The man gets to walk away and start again."

"I didn't do that!" Joel said, his voice rising. "I never walked away from you and started over with another woman. There is no girlfriend in Ohio! There never was!"

"But if you wanted to, you could," she countered. "You're free!"

"So can you," he retorted. "You might be unsure if you want to get to know that Oregon farmer, but he was interested. So don't pretend you have no options in life now. I know that Aaron complicates things for you." He pressed his lips together. "Let me correct that—*I* complicated things for you. Aaron wouldn't be here if it weren't for me. But you aren't stuck, Claire. Have you ever looked in a mirror?"

"Are you calling me a hypocrite?" She felt like the breath had been knocked out of her. After all these years of trying to do things the right way, even after her mistake, would he dare to say she was anything but honest about who she was?

"What?" Joel shook his head. "Claire, I asked if you've ever looked in a mirror, because you're beautiful! You're stunning, actually. You turn heads!"

"I do not." She stared at him, aghast. That wasn't the Amish way. Besides, if people looked at her twice, it was because she had a four-year-old boy in tow. "I am not out there preening, looking for male attention, I can assure you!"

"You most certainly do turn heads." Joel said it flatly, like a fact. "Maybe you don't like it. Maybe you don't notice. But you're gorgeous, and I know that I'm not the only one who sees it. There will be plenty of farmers who'd be more than willing to make you a wife. I assure you of that."

"Oh..." His compliment had taken the fuel out of her, and she looked up at him, searching around inside herself for the point she was trying to make.

"Are you going to do it, then? Are you going to write back to that farmer and tell him that you're interested?"

"I don't know," she said, a lump rising in her throat. "Like I said, you showing up made everything harder. I don't know if I can summon up the strength to write to a stranger and try to convince him he should vow to be mine for the rest of his days and let me be the one to care for him and his daughter."

"You deserve a good life." Joel's voice sounded wooden, as if he couldn't summon up the strength to encourage her in this, either.

"*Yah*, I do. But Joel, I know what it feels like to fall in love with a man and to have that happen spontaneously. I'm not an old maid who never experienced romance before. I have! And turning to a matchmaker who would find me someone appropriate felt like the right thing to do a few months ago. It felt like my solution."

"What changed?" Joel took a step closer.

"You showed up!" Why was he not understanding this? "You showed up on my door, and you always did tangle my heart up something fierce, Joel Beiler. I'm supposed to up and marry some stranger now? When I know what real love feels like?"

Joel was silent for a moment, and he caught her gaze with his simmering dark eyes. He licked his lips and looked like he was going to say something, then stopped.

Claire had said too much already, and she reached for the shovel again. This was why she should have come out here alone. Prayer and reflection could have helped her hold her tongue.

"Wait—" Joel caught her hand. "You said you know what real love feels like. Are you saying you loved me then, or you love me now?"

She shook her head. "Does it matter?"

"*Yah*, I think it does." His voice was low, deep, and it resonated through her like the toll of a bell.

She had most certainly loved him five years ago, and she'd worked hard to stop, because what did it get her? All it brought was pain! And then Joel showed up on her doorstep, and it was like all that hard work was ripped away, because falling in love with Joel had never been by choice. She couldn't help herself.

"Claire, then or now?" Joel pressed, and he stepped closer still, taking the shovel from her hands and then putting his hands on the sides of her face as he looked down at her. Her knees felt weak, and with the tickle of his breath against her face and his blazing gaze demanding the truth of her, she had no more strength to keep up appearances.

"Both," she whispered.

And his lips came down over hers in a searing kiss that made her heart nearly beat out of her chest. Yes, this was exactly what made it impossible for her to write letters with other men looking for a wife. A letter with a stranger felt cold and stagnant next to a kiss like this.

And she couldn't go a lifetime without this kind of love.

Joel hadn't meant to kiss her. He'd just needed his answer, and when she'd said she loved him, the kiss had been his response. Her lips on his felt like a homecoming—a frantic relief after too many years of trying to convince himself that she was locked in his past. Her cheeks were cool under his touch, but she moved closer, and he pulled her against his chest and closed his arms around her. This felt more right than anything in his life.

For five years, he'd been the image of chaste responsibility. He didn't flirt, he didn't take women out driving and he didn't respond to any hopeful interest from single women in Ohio. He hadn't been available—even though he was well and truly single. He'd been proud of his conduct, but bring him to Pennsylvania and into Claire's company again, and where did he find himself? Kissing her in a stable while the wind outside howled with the same intensity as his swirling emotions.

He pulled back and looked down at her plumped lips. Her eyes fluttered open, and he exhaled a shaky breath. He didn't let go of her, though. He never wanted to move from this spot again.

"I don't know if it's worth anything at all to you," he whispered, "but I love you, too."

"Oh, Joel..." Tears welled in her eyes, and she pulled out of his arms then, and he was forced to release her. But he caught her hand again, not willing to let go of all contact with her. He could feel the tremble of her pulse in her wrist, and he lifted her hand to his lips and pressed a kiss against it.

"I loved you when I first met you five years ago," he said against her fingers. "I loved you when I lay in that hospital bed, and I loved you with every heartbeat until now. But I shouldn't have come. I should have sent someone else."

"Why?"

"Because seeing you again—" His voice caught in his throat and he swallowed hard. "Because seeing you again is even harder than I thought it would be."

"*Yah*, I know that feeling." She smiled faintly and dropped her gaze.

Joel tugged her back into his arms, and she exhaled a long, shaky breath, as if she was feeling the same wild relief he did at holding her close. Five years ago, he'd felt strong and capable when he held her like this. But now, he was at a disadvantage. He used to have a lot to offer a woman—more than just a faithful heart.

"You haven't changed a bit," he murmured against her hair. And neither had his feelings for her. That was the tough part. He'd been praying that *Gott* would bring his emotions past her, let him see her in a more sisterly way, perhaps, but it was like *Gott* had laughed at that, because now he seemed to love her even more than ever. Now that all he had was this faithful heart, it was all in.

And that was not helpful!

"I certainly have changed." Claire pulled back. "I had a baby—that changes everything. I'm a *mamm* now."

"*Yah*, I know..." He swallowed. "Seeing Aaron, knowing that he's mine, that definitely changed me. Having a son in this world—Claire, I will do anything to take care of the two of you. That inheritance is yours. Anything else you need, you tell me, and I'll find a way to get it to you. I mean that. I'll provide for you until I can't anymore."

"Who will take care of *you*?"

"My *mamm*, for a little while, but I've already told her that we'll hire someone to come in and deal with me. She doesn't need to do that again. She did it once with my *daet*, and that's enough."

"So a stranger." Claire's tone betrayed her disapproval.

"It's better that way," he replied. "A stranger is paid to be there, and when they go home, they don't get hurt by what you say. You're just a job."

"And that's what you want to be?" She shook her head. "You want to be someone's job?"

"*Yah!*" Joel searched her face. Did she still not understand? "*Yah*, that's what I want. I don't want to crush anyone. I don't want to leave my family shaken and guiltily relieved that I'm gone! So *yah*, I've given it a lot of thought, and it's the best way to go."

"You've changed, Joel."

That stung to hear, even though he knew it was true. He was now physically half the man he used to be. A well-timed fib might soothe his ego, but it wouldn't do him any good in the long run.

"I know," he whispered. "And I'm sorry. Where does it leave us?"

"Where does it leave *you*?" she countered. "Because this doesn't really change anything for me except making moving on even harder than it's ever been! I'm still Claire Glick, Aaron's *mamm* and a woman people are starting to respect around these parts. But you—you're just passing through."

That wasn't fair, and he eyed her for a moment, wondering if she really believed that.

"I came to see you," he said. "You make it sound like I'm here on vacation. You know it's not like that."

"I know." She dropped her gaze.

"I wasn't just passing through your community five years ago, either," he said. "I meant to come back."

"But you didn't." She blinked back tears.

"I don't have to leave this time," he whispered. "I said it before. I could stay around here—start doing bookkeeping for some local businesses. I could be closer by..."

"My son's father, who can visit twice a week." She smiled bitterly. "A cordial relationship and some pleasantries over a piece of pie."

"Raising our son together."

She nodded, but there was no happiness in her face. She wanted more—every woman did. But he couldn't give it! He didn't have the strength a husband needed to provide!

"Claire, you know my situation."

"I know you didn't want me with you when you were sick."

"I'm still sick!" His voice started to rise, and he tried to lower it again, not wanting to scare her. "Claire, this is a condition I will die with. It won't go away. I won't heal from it. I will have stroke after stroke until one of them takes me. That's how this works."

"You don't know that! Where is your faith?"

"I saw it with my *daet*!" he shot back. "I know exactly what's waiting for me, but I'm going to be better than him—I'm not going to inflict that on a woman. Not on *any* woman, Claire. I'm not saying you aren't good enough. I'm not saying I prefer someone else. I'm saying, I'm not getting married. Period. That's got to mean something to you."

"If you stay, then I will never get married," she said, her voice tight. "If you stay here, I'll be your friend, and I'll be in love with you—which will be agony—and you will put a spotlight on me as the unmarried woman who is still friends with the father of her child. That will be juicy gossip, and that will make me completely unmarriageable."

Joel's presence wouldn't make her life any easier…even though staying here would soothe his heart. Being able to see her and Aaron, knowing they were okay—it would be a powerful relief for him. But this wasn't about him—he'd promised himself he wouldn't do that. There was more than one way to be a burden on a woman.

"So it's better if I leave," he said hollowly.

"I'm not telling you to stay away. But if you stayed, it would have to be discreet. And that starts to feel like deception, doesn't it? That level of discretion starts requiring lies."

"You're honest, and such a good woman," he said softly.

"That doesn't help me in the least if my reputation gets dragged through the mud again. I have to be practical, Joel. I have no other choice!"

"So loving each other as we do, there really is no way, is there?"

Claire's lips wobbled, and she blinked back tears.

"Claire, you've got to say it out loud," he said miserably. "Because I'm going to look back on this conversation a thousand times in the coming weeks, and I'm going to second-guess everything. I need to hear you say it clearly."

"There's no way," she whispered, and she wiped a tear off her cheek. "No matter how much I love you."

"Maybe after you're married, if your husband would allow it, I could visit Aaron sometime," he said, his voice husky. Was it even possible? Because she'd belong to another man then, and he'd be the one waiting for crumbs.

"Maybe." She swallowed. "But when Aaron is old enough, when he's baptized and he's already solid in the young man he's going to be, I can tell him who his real father is, and he can visit you—as a man. But not now."

If Joel was still strong enough to do it.

That was the hard part—he had no idea how the future would unroll, and he might very well miss his chance at getting to know Aaron as his son.

"Claire, I understand that it's best I stay away, but tell him I loved him, okay? Tell him that I had wanted to be a better *daet* to him and that I'd done my best. Tell him that—" Joel swallowed hard. "Tell him I loved his *mamm* dearly."

Claire nodded, and Joel bent down and pecked her lips. That would be the last kiss.

"I'm going to leave as soon as I'm able," he added.

She nodded and wiped tears off her cheek.

"In the meantime, you go on back inside," he said. "I'll finish up out here."

"But your leg—" she started.

"It'll hurt," he said roughly. "But let me be a man here—please."

Claire nodded and moved toward the door. He waited until she'd pushed it shut behind her, and then he let out a wavering sigh and picked up the shovel.

He'd clean up this stable and do what he could for her. When he left, he wanted her to have some proper memories of him, not some pathetic time when she'd taken care of him.

As he shoveled, with no one to see, the tears leaked down his cheeks. He might still be a man, but he had a heart to break.

Chapter Eleven

That night, the wind continued to blow, rippling across the pools of water and the swampy pastures and whistling past the half-submerged fence posts. It swept over Pennsylvania farmland, shrieked down chimneys and sucked up the moisture on the land below, shrinking the lake of water that drenched the front of the Draschel Bed and Breakfast. Muck was left behind where the water drained and evaporated, and some areas even dried up into cracked mud under the persistent blow of that howling wind.

Lying in bed that night, Joel listened to the moan outside and the rattle of the tin stovepipe, his own heart feeling like it could join in with the mournful gale. He'd come here knowing he wouldn't marry her. He knew it. And she had a future better than he could provide, if she'd just step out and claim it.

Maybe part of his penance would be watching her move on to a worthier man than he was. Even if it would hurt, and he'd carry it around with him as a perpetual ache inside his chest.

He finally did sleep, and it was a heavy, dreamless slumber. He awoke with a dry mouth and that dehydrated, empty feeling of heartbreak. It was like the last time he made this decision, propped up in a hospital bed, trying to slur out some semblance of his name for a patient nurse. He'd known then that he couldn't inflict this on Claire, and he'd had that same empty, dry-mouthed feeling. He'd thought it was the effect of the stroke. Maybe it had been more about heartbreak. Morning sunlight slanting through the window and pooling like gold on the wood floor didn't do anything to improve his frame of mind, either.

Gott, I love her, he prayed as he swung his legs over the edge of the bed. *And I love my son. I'm going to love that boy with everything I've got for as long as I live, but it's my feelings for Claire that are the problem, Gott. I love her, too, and I can't see that changing.*

Make me a good father for Aaron—somehow make a way. And help me to let go of Claire. She never was mine, and I'm still so sorry for having overstepped with her the way I did. In Your mercy, Gott, give me some peace.

He dressed, packed his bag and shaved with the pitcher of wash water Claire had left in his room. She had a kind heart—still caring for his comfort while knowing they'd never be more to each other. She was a very good woman, and she deserved a man who'd take care of her properly. If only that could have been him.

But *Gott* didn't make mistakes.

When he came out of his room, his bag in hand, no one was inside. Out the kitchen window he could see Claire and Aaron standing by the pool of water that still covered a large portion of the drive, and Ted and Gloria stood in borrowed rubber boots, the doors of their car open. The engine growled and then faded away. Ted emerged from the car.

There was still quite the flood, but he could see dry ground out by the road, and his horse and buggy would get through without any problems. It was probably for the best that he'd be able to leave, anyway. Staying here, knowing he could never be more to Claire, would be a different kind of punishment. Maybe Claire had been right about that.

He pushed open the side door and headed outside. Claire turned, and she fixed her blue gaze on him silently. He could see the depth of her sadness, and his first instinct was to march over there and pull her into his arms, but that wouldn't be right or proper.

"Good morning, Joel," Ted called. "I'm afraid our car won't start. The engine's flooded."

Joel tore his gaze away from Claire. "Is the fallen tree cleared?"

"I walked out to the road and I could see it. There's a bunch of men working on it with chain saws. It's almost all cleared away," Ted replied.

He could hear the distant buzz of those chain saws now that he paused to listen, but the twitter of birds was louder.

"My buggy will get through, then," Joel said.

Gloria emerged from the car then and looked at him hopefully. "Do you think you could drive us into town? If we don't call our daughter soon, she's going to be worried sick."

"*Yah*, of course," Joel said. "I'm happy to."

Ted and Gloria set about locking their car up again, and Claire walked over to where Joel stood, her arms crossed protectively over her stomach.

"You're leaving now?" she asked, her voice low.

"*Yah.* They need a ride, and—" He swallowed. "You didn't wake me."

"I thought you'd need the rest." She smiled faintly. "I'm sorry. It's not my business how much you rest, is it?"

"It's okay." He sucked in a slow breath, trying to tamp down the rising sadness inside him.

"I'll miss you, Joel."

And that didn't help. His heart felt like it would overflow, but there was no privacy for a proper goodbye, either.

"Me, too." He wanted to say more, but emotion closed off his throat.

Aaron came up then, the big German shepherd trailing loyally after him. Aaron looked up at Joel, then glanced at his mother. He frowned slightly.

"I'm heading out this morning, Aaron," Joel said, clearing his throat.

"Oh. Well, safe travels." Aaron sounded too grown up.

Joel and Claire both smiled at that. How many times had he heard that said to guests leaving this establishment?

"I want you to take good care of your *mamm*," Joel said.

"Oh, *yah*. I'm the man of the house." Aaron squinted up at him.

"You're the *boy* of the house, my dear." Claire smiled. "I still take care of you, not the other way around."

Right. Claire had a point. She was raising Aaron in her own way, and he'd often misstep when it came to how she wanted to handle things. Maybe this was just a gentle reminder that leaving was the right thing to do.

"Sorry," Joel murmured, glancing up to meet her gaze. Then he looked down at his son again. "I want you to do as your *mamm* says and always be extra nice to her."

"Okay." Aaron looked confused.

He couldn't say more. He couldn't hug Aaron or tell him he loved him. He couldn't hold Claire one last time, either. They had parts to play, and if Aaron wasn't going to know about him yet, then this would only make the boy uncomfortable. He was going to be Claire's secret, and it wasn't fair to expect her to stay as single as he was. She deserved the life he'd taken from her.

"Okay, well..." He cleared his throat again. "I'm going to go hitch up my buggy."

"I can give you a hand," Ted said cheerfully. "It's the least I can do in return for a ride."

"Aaron, I want you go inside and start your breakfast," Claire said.

"Now?" Aaron asked.

"*Yah*, now."

Joel had the urge to ask if Aaron could come help with the hitching, but this was Claire's call. She was his *mamm*, and she'd decide what was best.

"It was nice to meet you." Joel forced some cheer into his tone. "And nice to whittle cows with you."

"I'm going to make more cows!" Aaron said and then turned for the house. He hollered over his shoulder, "'Bye, Joel! 'Bye, Ted and Gloria!"

Joel led the way into the stable to get his horse, and hitching up didn't take long. His horse was antsy and ready to get moving again after being cooped up for the length of that storm. And when Joel had tightened the final strap, he helped Gloria up into the back of the buggy first.

"Do you want to…say goodbye with some privacy?" Ted asked, his voice low.

"No." He got up into the driver's seat and untied the reins. He'd said his goodbyes. There was nothing else to say, and the last thing he could express could only be said with a kiss. And he couldn't do that.

He leaned forward, and he saw Claire standing on the step, her hands clasped in front of her.

No, if he took one step toward her, he'd never leave again.

Joel leaned back, flicked the reins and silently prayed for strength. He was leaving his heart right here at the Draschel Bed and Breakfast.

Claire stood watching the buggy disappear down the drive, and she didn't know she'd been holding her breath until she sucked in a gasp of air. Joel was gone, and it hurt more than she thought it would.

She shut her eyes, and hot tears leaked past her lids, but she couldn't give in to this emotion. Not now. Inside the house, she heard the clatter of cutlery falling on the ground. Aaron was doing as she'd asked him to, but he wasn't very old yet, and things tended to slip out of his fingers.

Should she have let Aaron see the very last of Joel? She'd been afraid that Joel would say something, or that Aaron would finally notice that Joel was much more special than they'd been letting on.

"*Mamm?*" The door opened behind her, and she hurriedly wiped her eyes on her apron. "*Mamm*, are you okay?"

"*Yah*, son. I'm just fine."

"Are you crying?"

"No, no…not me. Something's in my eye. Did you get your breakfast?"

The wind picked up again and swirled around her legs, whipping her dress against her knees. It worked a tendril of her hair free from her *kapp*, and she had to duck her face against it. When the wind finally abated, the buggy was out of sight.

"I got cereal. Do you want cereal with me?" Aaron asked.

"No, Aaron. I'm not hungry." She wouldn't have been able to choke down a bite of food if her life depended on it.

"After I eat my cereal, can we go see the big tree that fell?"

"It's going to be chopped up by now," she said. "Or almost all chopped up."

"Then we better hurry!" Aaron said eagerly.

The phone booth was in the same direction they'd walk if they went to see the fallen tree, and she picked up the flyer from the counter where she'd left it.

"Son—" Claire sighed. "Son, we need to go to the phone booth, too. We have to call Ollie's owners."

"Do we?" Aaron deflated. "Maybe we can do that tomorrow."

But she didn't have the strength to put off any more difficult tasks. If she left this for tomorrow, she might very well curl up in bed and give in to her sadness, and that would not do. One foot ahead of the other—that was how a woman got through hard times. Every storm eventually ended—wasn't that what her *daet* always told her? Every storm…even this one in her heart.

"You know we do." She met his wide-eyed gaze. "Sometimes we have to do something that is right, even if it hurts."

Aaron nodded. "Okay, we'll call them, too. But can we see the tree?"

"*Yah*, but eat your cereal first. Then we'll walk out to see the tree and make our phone call."

Aaron ate his cereal in big, dripping bites, and when he'd finished all but a few floating flakes, he put the bowl down for the dog to finish the last of the milk.

"Goliath can walk with us, can't he?" Aaron winced. "Ollie. Ollie can walk with us, right?"

The dog perked up at the sound of his real name, and possibly the word *walk*. He looked around hopefully. The dog had been cooped up with this storm, too.

"*Yah*, of course."

Within a couple of minutes, they were back outside, both in their rubber boots and coats. The sun shone warm, but the wind was chilly, and Claire walked through the water, trying not to splash her dress while Aaron did the opposite and did his best to splash as much as possible.

"The water will get in your boots."

"It's already in my boots." Aaron grinned.

"Are your socks wet?"

"Completely soaked!" he announced with pride.

Boys… What could she do? They carried on up the drive until they got to dry ground again, and Aaron's steps squelched as they made their way to the road. The field across the street looked marshy, but the road was dry now, and Claire led the way toward the sound of the chain saws. The sunlight was warm on her shoulders, but it wasn't much comfort.

She missed Joel—missed him like a missing limb. That wasn't right—she'd only just seen him again. And he didn't want a marriage with her. This wasn't supposed to hurt this much. It was supposed to be a rational decision that would be a relief, so why wouldn't her heart see that?

Sometimes a woman had to do the hard thing, too. Eventually, when Aaron was grown, she'd put him in touch with his father. She'd tell him that Joel had loved him, and she might very well incur the anger of her only child. But right now, Aaron didn't need any more confusion in his life, and a stepfather might be good for him.

He'd need to learn how to be a man from someone.

There was a big pile of tree limbs and scraggly branches to one side of the road, and there was a lane cleared now as the team of *Englisher* men continued sawing up the thickest part of the trunk. They wore hard hats and blue jeans, and they had matching coats with a business's logo on the arm. Aaron stopped well back, watching them as the chain saws dug into the wood. Ollie sat next to him, ears up, back straight—a loyal friend.

Claire was going to send away more than a father today. She'd also have to send this dog back to his proper family. It was the right thing to do—there was no question! But she still felt a wave of maternal guilt.

Denying herself was fine. She was used to this. But denying her son a childhood of knowing his father…was *that* the right thing to do? Was a stepfather and a good reputation really better than his real father and the community watching her shame? Was she looking at what was right for her son or what was right for herself? The two would not always be the same. Joel was her ex, but he was Aaron's *daet*. A wriggle of uncertainty started inside her stomach.

The chain saws whined as they bit into the tree trunk, and Claire smoothed the flyer against her middle.

Gott, lead me, she prayed. Because she had no idea anymore what was the right path. Everything hurt—everything.

* * *

The horse seemed glad to be on the open road again, and he trotted along, his head and tail high. Gloria sat in the seat behind him, and Ted was at Joel's side. The couple seemed to be enjoying the drive. The fresh air normally did Joel some good, too, but not today.

Some of the fields were still flooded, and Joel could only assume it would be a while before herds would be getting back to those pastures again, but as soon as they dried out, the fields would flourish once more. All that extra silt and water had a way of sprouting new life. From destruction came fresh starts.

If only it was the same way for him. This was more than a storm in his life—this was the reality of it. It wouldn't get better, and he wouldn't be able to simply put Claire and Aaron into the past. That little boy was his son—his only son. The only child he'd have. And Claire…if he was going to let her go, he'd have done it long ago. He'd had ample reason and ample time. She wasn't going to be dislodged from his heart ever, was she? She'd stay right here with him, and he'd just keep on loving her.

Joel reined the horse in at a four-way stop and waited while a truck lumbered past them.

Gloria was in the seat behind, murmuring about the beautiful scenery, and Ted sat next to him, seeming to be caught up in his own thoughts.

The Wassels had had a hard last few days, too, with the anniversary of their son's death. Life wasn't easy for anyone, was it? Rain fell on the Amish and the English alike.

When the intersection was clear again, Joel flicked the reins.

"You're in love with Claire," Ted said, breaking the silence.

Joel looked over at him. "What?"

"You are." Ted met his gaze. "How come you left like that? She's just as in love with you. Watching the two of you part gave me a stomachache. I've been sitting here trying to keep my mouth shut because it isn't my business, and I know that, but..."

"Why *did* you leave like that?" Gloria finished the thought from the seat behind him.

So the *Englisher* couple hadn't been wrapped up in their own troubles. They'd been wrapped up in his. That was a frustrating thought. He didn't need curiosity. He just needed to find a way to shoulder this burden—get his balance.

"I, uh—" Joel swallowed. "I'm not the right

one for her. That's all. Don't worry yourself over it."

"I am a little worried about it, though," Ted said. "I just spent several days with you both, seeing you meet your son for the first time. That was powerful."

"*Yah.*" And it was private. It wasn't his fault he'd had an audience.

"Did she tell you that?" Ted asked. "That you aren't the right one for her?"

"No." Joel sighed. "This looks bad on me, I know. But it's more complicated."

"It always seems that way. Sometimes talking about it helps," the older man replied.

A chilly wind blew in the cracked window, and Joel licked his lips. Ted was right—it wasn't his business. But then, Joel had watched this couple go through pain of their own during the storm. And something inside him wanted to explain, to show that he wasn't some lazy man refusing to care for the woman he loved and the child he'd fathered.

"I've got a medical condition that will only get worse," he replied. "I don't want to be a burden on Claire. Or on Aaron. I know what that feels like—my *daet* had the same condition, and he made us all miserable."

He never wanted Aaron to feel that guilty

swell of relief when he eventually died, too. He couldn't do it.

"It might not be that bad for you," Ted said.

"And then again, it might." Joel glanced over at the older man. "A husband is supposed to be his family's protector. I can't be the man Claire would need me to be. It's better to face reality than disappoint her after it's too late. There is no divorce for the Amish. If I'm going to set her free, it has be now."

"You were so patient and understanding with your son," Gloria said quietly. "Not everyone is that good with small children."

"Give it time," Joel said ruefully. "I've been on good behavior."

Give it time, and he'd be laid up with another stroke—even a small one would take away from his current abilities. He'd be going to physiotherapy again, trying to relearn how to touch his face or how to lift a cup of water to his mouth. He'd need to be cared for like a baby—and his family deserved better than that.

"What do you do for a living now?" Ted asked.

"I'm a bookkeeper."

"Oh, that's great! Very much in demand, I imagine," Ted said.

"*Yah.* It's turning out to be a good choice. Thank *Gott.*"

"And bookkeeping wouldn't provide for a family? When you said protecting your family, I thought you meant fighting a bear or something!" Ted laughed at his own little joke.

"The income will be enough, and I'll be sending her money," Joel said. "But we Amish have men's work and women's work. The men's work is physical. It's outdoors—fixing fences, building chicken coops, breaking ground for a new garden…the list is endless—and physically demanding."

"Fixing the shingles?" Ted raised his eyebrows.

"*Yah.* That, too. I don't have the strength for it anymore. Look what happened when I tried. It's embarrassing. I can do some, but…what kind of husband leaves men's work for his wife to do while he sits indoors with a fire and a stack of ledgers?"

"You could ask for help," Ted said.

Joel cast him an annoyed look. "This hurts me more than anything, Ted. Trust me, I've examined all the angles. Are there ways to get things done? Yes. But Claire deserves better than my mother got."

"Hmm."

Gloria remained silent. Did she understand his perspective, at least? A woman could only take so much, and Claire might appear as strong as steel, but that didn't mean that she was. Or that she should try to be.

"I'm sixty-nine," Ted said quietly.

"Oh." Joel looked over at him, wondering why he'd been given this gift of information.

"I've been married for forty-seven years," Ted went on. "And I'm getting old."

"You look in good shape to me," Joel replied.

"Well, you haven't heard the sounds my back makes when I get up after sitting too long in the wrong chair." Ted grinned.

Joel didn't have it in him to smile back, and Ted's expression softened.

"I'm aging, Joel," Ted said. "I don't even talk to Gloria much about this, but I notice it in a lot of things, from how long I can walk before I get winded to how late I can eat my dinner without being kept up half the night with heartburn. And it gets at a man's ego, in a way. In my head, I'm young. I used to run marathons."

"That's impressive."

"I don't run them anymore," Ted qualified.

"My body can't take it. I know people my age who still hit the pavement, but I can't do it."

"No shame in that."

"Thanks." Ted smiled ruefully. "But after forty-seven years, I can assure you I'm a different man now than I was when I married Gloria. I'm no longer young and fit. If I was called upon to pick up my wife, toss her over my shoulder and run her to safety—" Ted looked over his shoulder toward his wife "—we'd both perish."

Gloria burst out laughing. "It's the truth."

"People get older." Joel flicked the reins, giving the horse some encouragement. "There's no shame in that."

"I'm still a man, though," Ted said. "Inside me, I still need to be the one my wife can lean on. I still want to be the answer to her problems, and I still want to make her heart flutter—in the good way, not the medically inconvenient way at our age."

Joel smiled at that little joke in spite of himself. "*Yah, yah...*"

"And over the years, I've learned that I bring much more to our relationship with some life experience and some wisdom. The biggest support I can be to my wife is not a physical one but an emotional one. Talking about our feelings, about our heartbreak and the hopes we still have for the future—that does more for our relationship than me still being able to run a marathon, you know?"

Joel nodded.

"People get old," Ted went on. "And we men are told that we need to stay tough, but that's not possible. Age gets us all in the end. Gloria and I help each other. You haven't seen teamwork until you've seen us try to cross our icy driveway and not fall, clinging to each other as we go. And we're closer now than we ever were before. It's funny how that works—relying on each other does it."

"But Claire wouldn't be relying on me as much as I would on her. It wouldn't be fair."

"Don't kid yourself," Ted replied. "Aaron's father talking that boy through life's challenges? That's priceless. A husband to hold her on a chilly evening? That's worth more than you think. Someone to love her for who she is, to think she's beautiful no matter what, even when she gets older and her hair goes gray—that means the world to the right woman."

"It does," Gloria murmured.

Joel looked over at Ted, imagining that kind of love with Claire. It would be effortless for him to love her like that, but would she want what life might bring with his illness? Was that kind of marriage possible with his condition?

"She might end up having to take care of a man ailing much faster than she does," Joel said.

"And she might find that to be an honor if she loves you enough," Gloria said. "Have you asked her?"

"Would she respect me still?" he asked, more a question to himself, although it came out aloud.

"My husband is twice the man now that he ever was when he carried me across the threshold of our first home," Gloria said. "My respect for him has to do with his character, his integrity, his wisdom gained through years of hard work. Our love has deepened over the years, and if you and Claire could find a way to a more mature, deeper relationship sooner, I don't see that as a liability. That would be a strength."

Joel had seen the worst that his father had put his mother through, but the thought of being there for Claire—in whatever way he could—had sparked some hope inside him. Could he be the man she spoke of the way

Gloria spoke of Ted? Maybe Joel had more to offer Claire than he thought. But he'd have to be sure…

Was his beating heart enough? Was his devoted love as valuable to her as these *Englishers* suggested?

They were almost at town, and a car eased past them, followed by another.

"It's something to think on." Joel didn't want to say too much, because he wasn't even sure if he was being foolishly hopeful right now or not. "I can drop you off at a hotel, if you want. They'd have a phone, and you could call a tow truck if you need one for your car and sort things out."

He was trying to change the subject now, because this was too personal to banter about. He had to think it through.

"That would do nicely," Ted said. "Thank you very much, Joel. It was a pleasure getting to know you."

Ted seemed to sense that this sharing time was over, but Gloria leaned forward, not to be put off.

"Joel, where will you go after you drop us off?" she asked.

"To the bank," he said. "I have some business to see to."

He'd promised Claire that money, and no matter how this went, it was hers. But he also meant to put a stop to this overly personal conversation. He was starting to feel like there might actually be a chance for him to be with Claire, and that thought was too enticing not to examine closer. But he needed privacy to do it.

Gloria sighed, and Joel glanced back at her. She looked out the window, and her eyes lost that earlier sparkle. He'd hurt her feelings, and he hadn't meant to. Was he becoming a gruff, mean man already? He certainly hoped not. He could do better than his father had.

"And then I'll go back to see Claire," Joel added. "I'll talk to her."

A smile broke over Gloria's face. "That's what I wanted to hear. I'm going to be praying for you, Joel. You can be sure of it."

And that did make him feel a little bit better.

Chapter Twelve

The Englishers had been thrilled to hear that Ollie had been found. The woman even shed a few tears over the phone and told Claire a few tricks to try, just to make sure it was him. He could shake a paw, roll over and he even played dead when a finger gun was pointed at him. Claire hadn't approved of that trick at all, but of course Aaron had loved that one the most.

It was hard to raise an Amish child without these outside influences, but she was doing it, wasn't she? She might be a single mother, but Aaron was polite, eager to please and very good at doing his chores. Aaron was her proof that she hadn't failed at all—she was doing the job of two people together, and her boy was turning out just fine. And yet, she still had that wriggle of worry that Aaron would resent her for this secret later.

When they got back to the house, Aaron went to play with his wooden farm in the sitting room, and Ollie lay in a pool of sunlight, watching him.

"Bang!" Aaron said from the other room. He was getting the dog to play dead.

"Aaron, I told you already!" Claire rose her voice to be heard from the kitchen. "We do not play guns! Ever. I don't care how fun the trick is, we do not pretend to kill those we love. Do you understand me?"

"Yah, Mamm."

Claire sat down at the kitchen table, a fresh piece of paper in front of her. Her gaze stayed on the doorway that led to the sitting room for a moment longer, waiting to see that Aaron was obeying. He was. The sounds from his playing turned to cattle rustling.

The letter must be written. She couldn't just put it off until she felt like responding. She'd asked Adel to serve as her matchmaker, and after lying awake half the night and saying a heart-wrenching goodbye to Joel, she knew beyond a shadow of a doubt that she would not move to Oregon and marry this worthy farmer, no matter how nice he was.

She couldn't do it. Her heart would never fully commit to that plan, and Adam Lantz in

Oregon deserved better. So did she. She deserved a man she could give her entire heart to, and that might not be possible for a very long time considering how she felt about Joel still.

Dear Adam,

I asked our local matchmaker to find me a husband, and I'm sorry to tell you that I was too quick to do so. I should have looked deeper in my heart to see if I was ready, and I truly am not. I hope I haven't wasted too much of your time, and I do hope that you find a wonderful and worthy woman to marry.

So I am sorry for this, but I must remove myself from your consideration.

She paused, looking at the last line. It felt… professional. Like she was turning down a job or pulling a résumé. It certainly didn't feel like a woman explaining herself to a potential suitor. But how else was she supposed to say it?

She heard the sound of hooves splashing through the water outside, and her heart skipped a beat. She went to the window and spotted an incoming buggy. But the driver wasn't Joel, as she'd been hoping. It was her friend Sarai.

Claire rubbed her hands over her face. This wasn't a good day for a visit. She didn't have her emotions under control, and she hated putting that on display. But still, it would be good to see a friend.

She opened the side door and waited while Sarai reined in the buggy on dry ground. She hopped down and waved.

"Claire! We were worried about you out here!" Sarai called, and she went around to the back of the buggy and pulled out a crate. "I brought you a few things to carry you through."

"You shouldn't be out driving on those roads!" Claire put her hands on her hips and forced a smile.

"Blame my *mammi*." Sarai carried the crate up to the door and Claire stepped back to let her inside. "She wouldn't rest until she knew that I'd checked in on you."

Sarai put it on the table, and Claire looked at the contents. There were some canned preserves, a loaf of bread, a shoofly pie and half a cured ham.

"Your *mammi* Ellen is just the sweetest,"

Claire said, giving her friend a hug. "Thank you. I'll put some tea on. How are you doing?"

"Oh, I'm fine. Life is just as ordinary as can be. What I wouldn't do for some excitement."

"Be careful what you wish for," Claire replied ruefully.

Sarai pulled the letter on the table closer and bent over it. Claire winced. Sarai didn't seem to have a sense of privacy at all, but that was just the way she was. Besides, she knew about the letter from Oregon.

"You're not sending this!" Sarai exclaimed.

"I am."

"No! I'm serious, Claire. You've got to think about it more. You don't have to marry him, but you could at least look into what kind of man he is. If you just toss him aside after all the work Adel did to find you a match, she might not consider you again when she's matching people up. She's got to consider her own reputation as a matchmaker, too, you know."

"I know. And I don't want to make Adel look bad. That's the furthest thing from my intentions. But maybe she shouldn't be considering me for a long while."

"Where is this coming from?"

Claire left the tea things and came back to the table. She sank into a chair next to her friend and sighed. In some ways, even though they were close to the same age, Sarai felt younger. She simply hadn't endured as much as Claire had. But Claire would try to explain.

"When the storm hit, I had three guests here. There was an *Englisher* couple who'd come for basket weaving and got stuck here when the tree fell, and..."

"And?"

"And another man arrived at my door in the downpour. He couldn't get out, either."

"Do I know him?" Sarai whispered, eyes wide.

Claire shook her head and lowered her voice to a whisper. "No. It was Joel Beiler, my son's father."

Sarai's jaw dropped, and Claire quietly told the story of Joel's arrival, their time together and how Claire had fallen in love with him all over again.

"I'm no longer a woman who was done wrong, Sarai. I mean, he did leave me, but he's not gone still. He came back, and while he won't marry me, he will help me financially. I'm not adrift on my own. I can't present myself in that way anymore. And I can't pretend that Joel isn't Aaron's *daet*. He loves him, Sarai. If you'd seen him with Aaron..."

Her son appeared in the doorway.

"Hi, Sarai!"

"Hi, Aaron." Sarai held her hands out to him and gave him a hug. After a little conversation with him, Claire ruffled her son's hair.

"Off to play, Aaron. Either that, or I'm going to get you to sweep the floor."

That always worked, and he bounded off to his toys again.

"But you both love each other!" Sarai whispered, taking up the conversation where they'd left it. "There has to be a solution!"

"If there is, I can't see it." Claire's gaze moved in the direction her son had gone. "But I can't very well pretend I'm someone I'm not to a man looking for an honest wife. I'd have to explain what happened, and... I'm not ready to do that."

"He might be very understanding." Sarai looked hopeful. "He knows that Aaron came from somewhere!"

"I also don't think I can give my heart, or my hand, to another man." Claire's voice felt thick with repressed tears.

Sarai sighed. "I'm sorry, Claire."

"It's okay." Claire swallowed. "We also found the dog's owners. They put out a flyer."

"Oh." Sarai frowned. "But Aaron was getting attached, wasn't he?"

"Sometimes we have to do the hard thing because it's right. That's what I've been telling Aaron, at least."

"I daresay the right thing for you, Claire, is to take care of the man you love," Sarai said. "So he's sick… Isn't that part of a marriage vow—in sickness and in health? If you love him, take care of him! Would you rather have another woman at his side when he's sickest again?"

Claire's heart clenched in her chest. "No! I wouldn't like that at all! But he won't budge on the issue. He doesn't want to make any woman go through the hardship his *mamm* went through with his *daet*. And he was such a strong man five years ago that his current state has him… I don't know…feeling like he isn't enough."

"Then show him that he is," Sarai said simply.

"How would I do that?" Claire spread her hands. "What am I supposed to do to show him that we could be a proper family?"

Sarai just shook her head. "If I were some relationship expert, I'd be married by now."

Claire smiled ruefully. "You and me both, Sarai."

They laughed softly, and Claire's gaze moved toward the doorway that led to the sitting room once more. She could hear Aaron's chatter to himself as he rearranged his cattle.

"I love him, Sarai," Claire said softly. "I love him because I can see him in my little boy, and I love him for the sweet, honorable man that he is. He really is the good man I knew him to be when I first met him. Sarai, I wasn't wrong about him! Do you know how hard that's been for me, thinking I was so naive and foolish to trust a man like Joel? I knew I shouldn't have overstepped in our relationship, but more than that, I thought I couldn't pick out a good man in a lineup, you know? I thought I was bad at seeing character. But it turns out that Joel was just as good and honorable as he seemed at first. He just thought he was doing me a favor by not weighing me down with a sick husband."

"Does he have a point?" Sarai asked softly. "Are you a little relieved to not have the responsibility of taking care of him?"

"No, he does not have a point!" Claire

retorted. "You were right when you said I wouldn't want anyone else caring for him when he needs it. I love him. But if he doesn't want me there when he's at his weakest, well, maybe that's a test of *his* love. Not mine. Maybe he's good and decent and honorable and...doesn't love me as much as he needs to in order to take those vows. I've seen people get married with absolutely no appreciation for the promises they make. They don't think about life's trials. They only think about life's blessings. So maybe this is best. He's seeing how hard life can be, and he's making a realistic choice."

Tears rose up in Claire's eyes, and she did her best to push them back, but they wouldn't stop, and they slipped down her cheeks.

"Oh, Claire." Sarai wrapped her arms around her, rocking her back and forth. "That's the biggest load of malarkey that I've ever heard."

"What?" Claire pulled back in surprise.

"I'm sorry, but it is. You love him. He loves you, and you both need a good kick in the backside to get you moving in the right direction. And that's all I have to say about that." Sarai was silent for a moment. "Actually, I have one more thing to say about that. My *mammi* tells me stories about her marriage to my *dawdie* before he passed away. And she said that the secret to a long and happy marriage is to know when to step back and let *Gott* get through to your husband for you."

"What?"

"Well, more precisely, she said that *Gott* has better aim than a wife ever does, and if your husband just won't listen, you go to your knees and you say, '*Gott*, please get through to him.' She said that every time she prayed that prayer, by nightfall, her husband would have come across something that opened his eyes to a new perspective."

"But Joel isn't my husband," Claire murmured. Was that a special blessing for married couples?

"*Gott* still has better aim than you do," Sarai said. "It can't hurt to try. Ask *Gott* to show Joel what you can't."

That evening after supper, the *Englishers* arrived for Ollie. They drove up in a mud-spattered SUV, and when Claire opened the door, the dog went rushing out at the sound of their voices and leaped into their arms. They hugged him, pet him, and then put him down on the ground, because a dog that big was rather heavy. But the joy was evident.

There was no need to question where Ollie belonged, and Aaron stood by Claire's side, his lip trembling and tears in his eyes.

"Can I say goodbye to him, *Mamm*?"

"*Yah*, son. Go ahead."

Aaron went over to Ollie's owners and sank to his knees in front of the dog. He wrapped his arms around his furry neck and held him close for a moment, then pulled back.

"'Bye, Goliath," Aaron said softly.

The dog licked the tears from his cheeks, and Aaron stood back up.

"I took good care of him." Aaron looked up at the *Englishers* earnestly. "I loved him, and I fed him and I let him sleep in my bed, too. And I know he must have missed you a lot, but I did my best for him."

"You are quite an exceptional young man," the woman said. "We'd like to give you a reward for taking care of him for us."

"No," Claire said quickly. "That isn't necessary."

"Do you have other dogs here?" the man asked.

"No, but after seeing how much my son

loved your dog, I think we'll be looking for a puppy," Claire replied.

The *Englishers* looked at each other and smiled.

"Ollie here is a purebred," the man said. "We have another dog, and we breed puppies. There's a new litter of five, and four are already spoken for. There is a little male pup who looks a whole lot like Ollie who's not taken yet. We normally sell them, but if you wanted a puppy, we'd be happy to bring that last dog for you once he's weaned."

Aaron's eyes grew large, and he whirled around to look pleadingly at Claire.

"Would you accept a puppy?" the woman asked.

"*Yah!*" Claire nodded with a grateful smile. "We'd love to adopt a puppy into our family. Thank you so much."

When Ollie and his family drove away, Aaron had a smile on his face, and Claire couldn't help but send up a silent prayer of thanks that *Gott* had provided a way to soothe her little boy's heart while he made the right decision.

May *Gott* send her some balm, too. She was going to need it.

But just after the SUV turned onto the

road, a horse and buggy made the turn into their drive. Claire shaded her eyes. Who was coming to see them now?

Joel flicked the reins, his heart lodged in his throat. He could see Claire and Aaron standing out in front of the house, and he suddenly had a wave of misgiving. What if he'd misread her? Did she really love him as much as he thought? Would she consider a future with a man who couldn't promise health and strength? Was he really going to ask her to?

But he was here now, and if Gloria was true to her word, he had at least one person praying for his success this afternoon. Joel reined in his horse and put a hand to his shirt, where he'd tucked a crinkling envelope. He was going to do right by her financially, at the very least. He hopped down to the ground, and Aaron beamed at him.

"Hi, Joel!" he called. "I'm getting a puppy! And he'll look just like Goliath!"

"*Yah?*" Joel smiled. "I'm glad to hear it." He glanced over his shoulder. "Was that the dog's owners leaving?"

Claire nodded and ruffled Aaron's hair. "Aaron, I want you to go inside and clean up your farm, okay?"

Aaron headed inside, and they stood in the warm afternoon sunlight together. From inside, she could hear Aaron settling in to play a little more instead of cleaning up, but she didn't really mind. As long as he was distracted.

"I—uh—" Joel's mouth was dry. "First of all, before anything else, I brought you the money. It's a certified check made out to you." He pulled out the envelope and handed it over. Claire accepted it but didn't open it.

"Thank you for this, Joel," she said softly. "You always were a decent man."

"Are you doing okay?"

"*Yah.*" She nodded quickly. "I'm good." But then tears welled up in her eyes, and her nodding turned into a head shake. "I'm not good. I'm not okay at all, Joel."

Joel wrapped his arms around her and pulled her close against him.

"What happened?"

"You happened!" she said against his shirt, then she pulled back. "Joel, when Gloria and I were talking a few days ago, she told me something that suddenly had some new meaning this afternoon."

"Oh?" Had she realized how much he'd hurt her all over again?

"Easter is coming."

"*Yah.*" He nodded.

"And for *kinner*, it's a time of springtime and baby animals," she said. "It's time for families to eat big meals together and to celebrate that He has risen." She licked her lips. "But when hard times come, those holidays that were filled with laughter and joy become more somber and much deeper. We realize the true gift of Jesus's death and resurrection when we are faced with our loved ones getting sick..." She lifted her gaze to meet his. "You don't want to be a burden to me, Joel. I know that. You think I'm not strong enough to handle taking care of you if you should have another stroke, and maybe you're right. I might not be. But do you know who is?" She looked upward. "Him."

"What are you saying?"

"I'm saying that you're choosing to be sick alone, and you don't have to. I've written a letter to Adam Lantz in Oregon. I'm not going to pursue getting to know him. My heart is already taken. It has been for five years."

Did she mean it? Joel searched her face, and she simply met his gaze, her expression calm and serene.

"Speaking of Ted and Gloria," he said quietly, "Ted told me what a husband offers a wife that isn't all brawn and physical strength. He talked about emotional strength and loving her as long as *Gott* gives them life and enjoying her beauty as the years slip by. Claire, I'm not the man I used to be, but I want to be that strong man so badly. I want to be the muscle that protects you and the strength that takes care of men's work. I want to be the man you look up to."

"I already do." Tears shone in Claire's eyes. "And I'm just going to tell you straight. If you hire some stranger to care for you when it should be me, I'm not going to forgive you!"

"It should be my wife." The last word stuck in his throat.

There was a beat of silence.

"*Yah*, if you had one."

"I couldn't see myself married to anyone but you." He breathed out.

Was she considering it? Was she thinking of how to let him down? She was silent for a few beats, and he realized he hadn't exactly asked her to marry him. Not in so many words, but it was what he'd meant.

"First of all, there'd have to be a wedding," she said at last.

"I can do that," he said hurriedly. "I can vow to be yours, if you'll vow to be mine. Claire, I'll do my best. I just can't promise my health. But I'll do my best."

"No one can promise health, Joel." Her voice stayed firm. "I can't promise it, either. That's in *Gott*'s hands. But I can promise to stand by you and take care of you, if you can promise to keep loving me and to do your best to be kind."

"*Yah!* I can promise that here and now." He caught her hands in his. "You have my heart—all of it. There's no one else for me. I love you so much it hurts, and I want to be a proper *daet* to Aaron. So… I'm going to ask officially. Are you ready?"

"Yah."

"Claire, will you marry me?"

She nodded, tears sparkling in her eyes. "*Yah*, Joel, I'll marry you."

He pulled her into his arms and lowered his lips over hers. She seemed to melt into his arms, and he held her close, inhaling the soft scent of her and memorizing her lips against his. She felt like home. She felt like comfort and hope. And may *Gott* give him the strength to stay kind to her, no matter how much frustration and pain came his way. Because she deserved nothing but kindness and happiness for every moment of her life.

When he pulled back, he spotted his son on the step, staring at them with a scowl.

"Sweetie." Claire laughed.

"How come you're kissing my *mamm*?" Aaron demanded.

"I'm—" Joel looked down at Claire. How would she want to handle this?

"Aaron, do you remember when we talked about you getting a *stepdaet* one day?"

"I don't want a *stepdaet*."

"What about your real *daet*?" Claire asked softly. "What would you think about getting to know him…and having him be part of our family?"

"My real *daet*?" Aaron looked between them.

"Let's go inside and talk about it." When Claire looked up at Joel, happiness shone in her eyes.

Aaron's real *daet* was coming home, and Joel was going to marry Claire and seal this deal just as quickly as was proper. They belonged together. There was nowhere else he wanted to be.

As they went up the steps together, arm in arm, Joel's heart swelled with gratitude. God had brought him back to the only woman he'd ever loved, and he couldn't believe the depth and the width and height of this blessing.

Make me worthy of her, Gott, he prayed. *Make me worthy.*

Epilogue

Claire and Joel went to see her cousin Bishop Glick together. Zedechiah—because she never could call him *Bishop* without feeling a little silly—was very pleased to hear that a wedding was coming. He shook Joel's hand heartily, and his wife, Trudy, gave Claire a big hug. Zedechiah told them that they had two options: get married with little fuss in his sitting room, or have a big, proper Amish wedding.

"Which do you want?" Joel asked her.

"I'm not sure," she admitted, and her stomach fluttered at the thought.

She longed to simply bring Joel home and not waste another minute apart. But she'd missed out on the wedding she'd hoped for, and there was a part of her that longed for a wedding apron and guests and games and all the joy that came with a community celebrating together.

"What do you want?" she asked him.

"I promised you a wedding, Claire," Joel said. "I'd like to keep my promise."

So they decided upon a proper Amish wedding to take place two months in the future. It gave Joel time to move to Pennsylvania and start his own bookkeeping business there with the references he'd secured in Ohio, and it also gave Claire a little more time with Aaron as she helped him to adjust to the idea of his *daet* living with them. Claire's parents and sisters were all happy for her, but they did take some convincing to trust Joel again.

"Time will tell," her father said soberly. "But after a wedding…there is no backing out, Claire. This is the rest of your life we're talking about, and you deserve a beautiful life."

"I've prayed about this, *Daet*," Claire assured him. "I'm certain."

But that didn't mean that Claire didn't have to go back to her Bible and pray repeatedly to have more reassurance from *Gott* that her heart wasn't leading her astray.

Those two months flew by. Claire's friends

pulled together to help her make her wedding dress, and the grandmothers of Redemption, led by Sarai's *mammi*, put their skills to good use and made a beautiful wedding quilt for the big day. Claire's friends Sarai and Naomi had agreed to stand as her *newehockers*, or bridesmaids. Naomi and her husband would travel back from Ohio for the wedding. Within a matter of weeks, all the details were brought together for a big Amish wedding.

Those five weeks before Joel returned were stressful for Claire, because she'd experienced Joel lovingly taking leave of her once before—and he hadn't come back. So this time, her stomach was in knots as she waited. But almost every day another letter arrived—short and to the point. Joel said it clearly—he loved her, and he couldn't wait to marry her. He was coming.

"This short separation isn't a bad thing," Adel told her gently. "It gives him a chance to do this properly—to come and settle down with you. If he doesn't...well, you have all of us to hold you up, and I'm still a matchmaker, Claire. Okay? Your life will not be over, I promise you that. But if you don't endure some waiting now and see him come back to you just like he said he would, you'll be in a panic every time he takes the buggy into town. And that's no way to live a life."

Adel was right—she tended to be. And when Joel came back and pulled her into his arms, she clung to him with relief. He would stay with Bishop Glick and his wife until they were properly wed. Adel also hired Claire as her permanent manager for the bed-and-breakfast, and she said she liked the idea of having a man around the place, too, just for Claire's safety. Claire, Joel and Aaron would live at the B&B and run it, and Joel could run his own bookkeeping business from there as well. Their start would be a smooth one.

Their wedding day was a warm May Thursday, and the Glicks hosted the big day on their farm. Aaron's puppy had arrived the day before, and he hadn't been quite so happy about this wedding as Claire had hoped he would be. Joel was his *daet*, but he didn't have those sweet memories that she had. So Claire agreed that he could bring little baby Goliath with him to the wedding, and bringing his puppy with him did cheer the boy up considerably.

Before the wedding ceremony started, Claire and Joel sat down with Aaron out by the buggies for a moment of privacy.

"We're going to be a proper family now," Claire said quietly. "How do you feel about all of this, son?"

Aaron just shrugged and hugged the fluffy little pup a little closer. Could Claire really go through this wedding today knowing her son wasn't happy? If only he could feel what she did…but Aaron was his own little person. And she'd been so certain she could bring him over to her way of seeing it by now. She looked up at Joel, and he gave her a reassuring smile.

"Maybe we should talk man to man," Joel said, squatting down. "I'm your *daet*, but you don't really know me very well, do you?"

Aaron shook his head, then shrugged. "I know you a little bit. You make nice cows."

Claire had known it would be difficult for Aaron when she married, but she'd hoped that it would be different with Joel.

"Here's the thing, Aaron," Joel said. "When two people get married, they make promises, and a marriage is just two people making promises and keeping them for their rest of their lives. But there's lots of different kinds of promises. In fact, when your *mamm* and I get married, I'm going to be making some promises to you, too. And those are just as important as the ones I make to your *mamm*."

"*Yah?*" Aaron squinted at Joel.

"*Yah,*" Joel said. "I'm going to take care of you two. I'm going to be kind to you. I'm not going to give you a hard time, Aaron. And I'm going to make sure your *mamm* is the happiest woman in Pennsylvania, and she wouldn't be if you weren't happy, would she?"

"Will you let baby Goliath sleep in my bed?" Aaron asked.

"Is that what you were worrying about?" Claire asked.

"You said you didn't know yet if he could!" Aaron turned big, teary eyes toward her. "And I heard Cousin Zedechiah say that a *daet* might have his own ways, and then Adel said that I need to learn to be a man from my *daet*, and, and I don't want to be a big man yet. I want to be a boy! And I want my dog!"

Little ones had big ears, and it seemed that for the last two months, Aaron had been listening to all sorts of conversations she'd thought were private.

"You want baby Goliath to sleep with you?" Joel asked quietly.

"*Yah!*" Tears welled in the boy's eyes. "I really do!"

"Well, it's fine by me if your *mamm* agrees," he said.

Claire smiled mistily. "I think that would be fine, too."

"Really?" Aaron asked. "You promise?"

"With all my heart, son," Joel said, and his voice caught. Claire wasn't the only one with tears in her eyes. "I'm going to keep my word. If your *daet* says it, you can count on it, okay, Aaron?"

Aaron nodded. "Okay."

Joel stood up, and Claire saw the tenderness in his gaze as he tapped the top of Aaron's straw hat. Joel looked over at her, and her heart filled with love for this gentle man who was determined to be strong in the only way that mattered.

He'd keep his word, and that was all she needed, too. What was a marriage but making and keeping promises for the rest of their lives, anyway?

"Are you ready now, Aaron?" Claire asked.

"*Yah*." Aaron slipped his free hand into hers.

"Let's go get married," Joel said.

Claire would be making her vows today, and with her vows came her trust, and her life, her future, her son…her everything.

Gott, bless us, she prayed in her heart. Because with just a teaspoon of blessing and two hearts determined to do right, she knew they'd be just fine.

* * * * *

If you enjoyed this Amish Country Matches story by Patricia Johns, be sure to pick up the first book in this series, The Amish Matchmaking Dilemma, *available now from Love Inspired!*

Dear Reader,

I hope you enjoyed the second story in my Amish Country Matches miniseries. If you enjoyed this book, I do have a backlist you could check out on my website at patriciajohns.com. All my books are sweet, emotional romances that you can trust not to go beyond a kiss. That's an author guarantee. Maybe you'll find more of my books you'll enjoy!

If you'd like to connect with me online, you can find me on Facebook, Twitter and Instagram. I'm always happy to hear from my readers, so reach out! You'll make my day.

If you'd like a chance to win a free book and a knitted surprise, sign up for my newsletter on my website. Not only will you get updates on my new releases, but I choose winners to receive packages from me every month, too. I hope you'll sign up!

And if you enjoy this book and leave a review, know that you've made an author truly grateful.

Until next time,
Patricia

COMING NEXT MONTH FROM **Love Inspired**

HIS FORGOTTEN AMISH LOVE

by Rebecca Kertz

Two years ago, David Troyer asked to court Fannie Miller...then disappeared without a trace. Suddenly he's back with no memory of her, and she's tasked with catering his family reunion. Where has he been and why has he forgotten her? Will her heart be broken all over again?

THE AMISH SPINSTER'S DILEMMA

by Jocelyn McClay

When a mysterious *Englisch* granddaughter is dropped into widower Thomas Reihl's life, he turns to neighbor Emma Beiler for help. The lonely spinster bonds with the young girl and helps Thomas teach her their Amish ways. Can they both convince Thomas that he needs to start living—and loving—again?

A FRIEND TO TRUST

K-9 Companions • by Lee Tobin McClain

Working at a summer camp isn't easy for Pastor Nate Fisher. Especially since he's sharing the director job with standoffish Hayley Harris. But when Nate learns a secret about one of their campers that affects Hayley, he'll have to decide if their growing connection can withstand the truth.

THE COWBOY'S LITTLE SECRET

Wyoming Ranchers • by Jill Kemerer

Struggling cattle rancher Austin Watkins can't believe his son's nanny is quitting. Cassie Berber wants to pursue her dreams in the big city—even though she cares for the infant and his dad. Can Austin convince her to stay and build a home with them in Wyoming?

LOVING THE RANCHER'S CHILDREN

Hope Crossing • by Mindy Obenhaus

Widower Jake Walker needs a nanny for his kids. But with limited options in their small town, he turns to former friend Alli Krenek. Alli doesn't want anything to do with the single dad, but when she finds herself falling for his children, she'll try to overcome their past and see what the future holds...

HIS SWEET SURPRISE

by Angie Dicken

Returning to his family's orchard, Lance Hudson is seeking a fresh start. He never expects to be working alongside his first love, single mom Piper Gray. When Piper reveals she's the mother of a child he never knew about, Lance must decide if he'll step up and be the man she needs.

LOOK FOR THESE AND OTHER LOVE INSPIRED BOOKS WHEREVER BOOKS ARE SOLD, INCLUDING MOST BOOKSTORES, SUPERMARKETS, DISCOUNT STORES AND DRUGSTORES.

LICNM0423